OF FLESH & BONE

TENEBRIS: AN OCCULT ROMANCE, BOOK TWO

KATHRYN ANN KINGSLEY

Copyright © 2022 by Kathryn Ann Kingsley

ASIN: B0B1GXQCBS

Paperback ISBN: 9798839336025

KATHRYN ANN KINGSLEY

All rights reserved.

No part of this book may be reproduced in any form or by any electronic or mechanical means, including information storage and retrieval systems, without written permission from the author, except for the use of brief quotations in a book review.

This is a work of fiction. Names, characters, places, and incidents either are the product of the author's imagination or are used fictitiously, and any resemblance to locales, events, business establishments, or actual persons—living or dead—is entirely coincidental.

A WARNING

This story contains content that may be upsetting to some readers, including torture in the form of LGBTQIA+ conversion "therapy," murder, madness, and consensual relations with monsters that involves the enjoyment of fear.

CHAPTER ONE

Professor Raphael Saltonstall was about to commit murder.

It was an action that was admittedly not new to him. He had done it countless times already, but at least it had always been for practical reasons. That was something he took great pride in. Every soul who met their end by his hand—or the infestation that lurked inside the darkness that surrounded him—had done so because it had served a purpose.

He had never murdered out of anger. Never out of revenge, or jealousy, or petty greed. Nor did he kill for joy or sadistic pleasure. He felt nothing at the death of those who died at his hands, save a modicum of regret.

The way a farmer would think about putting down their livestock, perhaps. Sadness at the loss of life, but there was no other practical solution. Sometimes death was necessary.

Rafe turned the closed pocketknife over in his palm where it was concealed in his coat as he stared at the entrance to the nightclub called the Flesh & Bone and reminded himself of his mantra.

He only killed when it was required. When someone needed to be removed for the purposes of the Society he served. Or when his infection was starving and needed to be fed.

But tonight was different.

Tonight's murder served a purpose, yes. The young woman was dangerous and had the potential to cause great harm beyond the measure that he fully understood. He knew why the Idol believed she played some important part in their plans, and he and the rest of the Mirror had long since vowed to foil them at every turn.

Emma Mather had to die before she became a pawn in their game.

Let alone all the chaos and destruction she could wage upon Arnsmouth, or more, if the other powers in the city got their hands on her. But there was another reason she had to meet her end—namely, because he didn't *wish* to kill her, and that made her a weakness. A weakness that he could not afford to keep, yet he wasn't quite certain he could bring himself to rid himself of.

Yet it might not matter. He had tried once before to kill her and opted instead to remove her memories to spare her life.

Cringing, he shut his eyes and let out a breath.

Her laughter haunted him like a ghost. Her smile had warmed a part of him, and her presence, short as it had been in his life, had comforted a loneliness in his soul. He had been given shelter against the cold night, and now that he found himself back out in the chill, he was all the more miserable for it.

She had shown him a very brief glimpse of companionship, and it had stained him in a way that he deeply regretted. But no matter how hard he tried to ignore it, like a spot of blood on a carpet, it was no use. He kept being dragged back to her. Nothing he tried had kept his thoughts from returning to her at the strangest times.

Or every time he sat at his desk.

Damn it all.

She was a blazing light in the darkness, unafraid to touch the most horrifying parts of him. The fact that she not only seemed immune to the unending bloodlust of his infection, but instead seemed *fascinated* by the Things that had corrupted him…it almost gave him hope.

No. She had to die for one very good reason that he found both practical and offensive.

Emma Mather had to die.

Because she had become a weakness.

Emma had made a terrible mistake.

Deep down inside, she knew what she was doing was a very bad idea. The problem was, she couldn't remember *why*. And that was the only reason she let her feet go one in front of the other, as she was half-pushed, half-led through the crowded nightclub.

She had gone into the Flesh & Bone.

And now she had the distinct sensation that she was about to die.

The jazz club that rushed by Emma was a blur of glitter, feather boas, long pearl strings, and the smell of cigarette smoke. Every now and then she caught the whiff of alcohol or the particular musk that came along with drugs.

It all made her dizzy. The hot air of the club and the press of people and loud conversations was in stark contrast to how cold she had been out in the rain, and how soaked through she still was. She was freezing. But she was also too hot at the same time.

What also didn't help was the fact that she knew, just *knew*, she was being ushered through the jazz club by a man she distinctly disliked. Mykel, the man with the bright white suit that contrasted sharply against his dark skin, had a smile she simply didn't trust.

By the time Mykel pushed her through a door into the back room, she was almost ready to collapse. Or shoot someone. Or both, in either order. She wasn't a picky individual. Or at least she didn't think she was.

Emma very much hated missing her memories. But that was why she was here, and that was why she was willing to put her life on the line and walk into what she was certain was a snake den. Because someone, or some*thing*, had robbed her of her life. And she wanted it back.

Or she wanted them to pay. Or both, in either order.

"You poor, poor thing! Get her a towel, will you, Anastasia? No—that's a *scarf*, you intolerable piece of Bakelite! Go to the kitchen and get something out of the back!" The woman who had spoken threw their arm around Emma, pulling off her coat and purse before Emma could get out even a single word. The same hands pushed her down into a chair.

It wasn't until she was sitting that she realized she had been close to fainting. The world was spinning around her as she struggled to get her bearings, and it took everything she had not to be sick.

"Look at you! So pale. You haven't slept a wink in all these months, have you?" The voice sighed heavily and stroked a hand over Emma's soaked hair. "And were you just standing out in the rain all day? You're drenched!"

Finally, she had the strength to look up. The woman before her looked the opposite of how Emma felt. In fact, the lady who was fussing over her was quite simply the most beautiful woman Emma had ever seen. Or had remembered seeing. *I really fucking hate this.* "I...think I might have been, actually. Standing out in the rain, I mean." The fact that she hadn't been sleeping was also true, but she figured that was fairly obvious by the bags under her eyes. She wiped a hand over her face. "I'm sorry. I must look a mess."

The woman tutted. She had blonde, perfectly curled hair that came down to her jawline. She was dressed in a slinky, clingy sequined dress that was just pushing the barriers of what was socially acceptable with its plunging neckline and slit up the thigh. But she wore it like a second skin, and Emma couldn't imagine her wearing anything less than something that daring. It suited her perfectly.

Taking a breath, Emma went into the same speech she had given everyone she had met in the past six months. "I'm sorry if I don't remember you, but—"

"Oh, shush." The woman frowned with perfectly painted crimson lips. "I know. You don't need to explain. That *bastard* did this to you." Her expression contorted to one of anger before smoothing again. "But we'll make it right, hm?" She placed her palm against Emma's cheek. "You're all right, now."

Another young woman entered the room meekly, holding a stack of towels. She was dressed like a showgirl, wearing less than she probably should be. But it was a jazz club, after all.

"Finally!" The lead woman snatched the stack of towels and set them down on the dressing table that ran the length of the wall next to them. It was spanned with mirrors and bright lights, meant for the performers to be able to put on their makeup and outfits in the perfect conditions.

Oh, I'm in a dressing room. Huh. I really must not be feeling well. Emma shivered as the cold from her wet clothes hit her again. The blonde in front of her unfurled one of the towels, draped it around Emma's shoulders, and then offered her a second.

Emma smiled faintly in return and began to dry herself off. "Thank you."

"Mykel is fetching you dry clothes. I know he rubs you the wrong way—I don't blame you, he tends to come off strong—but he's loyal. A good man." The blonde smiled. "My name is Gigi, and we're good friends. I promise. You don't have to be scared here."

"I get the feeling this place is dangerous." Emma shook her head. "All I have to go on are my gut instincts." She began to dry her hair, glad for the simple comfort of it. "Not that I don't believe you."

"This place is extremely dangerous. You're right." Gigi chuckled. "But you're still safe with me. I won't lie, when you first came to town, I was ready to put you in a ditch. Oh, don't give me that look!"

Emma was wondering how else she was supposed to respond to being told that she had plotted her murder, but fine. She went back to drying herself off.

Gigi didn't seem to take it personally. "There's a lot at stake, you know, here in Arnsmouth. A lot of very careful schemes that play out in the shadows. And you and your brother came in and ruined them all."

Mykel entered the room, flashed a grin to Emma, and set a stack of clothes on the dressing table. "For the wet pussycat."

Emma narrowed her eyes at him. "I wish you wouldn't talk."

"I know." He laughed as he left, shutting the door behind him.

Gigi was chuckling as well, smiling at her with an expression that was both saddened and amused. She scooped up the clothing and handed it to Emma, before gesturing to a screen in the corner of the room. "Change out of those soggy clothes, strawberry, before you catch a cold."

"Might be too late for that." She stood from the chair, eager at the idea of not being so soaked. Stepping behind the screen, she started stripping out of her dress and stockings, kicking aside her damp shoes. She'd have to let those air out. "Thank you."

"Of course. You have impeccable timing. I just ended my set for the night. We have a few hours before the place closes down for the morning." Gigi was rustling about on the other side of the screen. For all Emma knew, she could be getting a gun to murder her with. But something told her that for now, Gigi was telling the truth that she was safe. "Are you hungry? I'll get the kitchen to whip something up. Anastasia!" she called, likely out of the doorway. "Get her some dinner, will you? And *stop* picking your nose, for the last time!" The door shut with a click. "Sweet girl. An idiot, but a sweet girl."

"I'm starving," Emma said with a laugh. "I don't think I've eaten in…I don't know. A while." Maybe Gigi really *was* a friend.

"What's going on, hun? I know what he did—or at least the jist of it. But you look like a ghost."

"I feel like one." She pulled the new dress on and zipped it up the side. It was a little bit too big for her, but not enough to be a problem. The undergarments had fit just fine. It was just such a relief to be dry. "I don't…I don't know how to describe what it's like. I don't know who I am. I don't know who I'm supposed to be. People keep telling me, I see these photos of myself, but it's all gone. That girl is gone."

"I've never had one of those bastards rummage around in my head and take what they want." The other woman huffed. "Men. Always feel like they're entitled to everything, don't they?"

"I guess." When Emma came around the screen, Gigi was lounging on a sofa by the wall. She patted the cushion next to her. With a shrug, not knowing what else to do, Emma walked over and sat beside the beautiful blonde.

Gigi wrapped an arm around her and pulled her into a hug. "You aren't gone, Emma. You're right here. You're alive, and you're safe, and we'll get your head back on straight. Somehow." She chuckled. "Even if I have to rip his fucking fingernails off with a pair of pliers."

Emma stared at the blonde for a moment. Gigi had said the threat with such a casual air that it gave Emma zero doubts that she meant every word. Which was both terrifying and yet weirdly made Emma like the woman even more.

She didn't know what that said about her, but there it was. "Who did this to me? Do you know?"

"Of course." Gigi reached out and stroked a hand over Emma's damp hair. "His name is Professor Raphael Saltonstall. He is a member of the Dark Society known as the Mirror. You fell in with him while searching for your brother, Elliot. You should've sided with me, but..." Gigi smirked. "You and he had rather a bit of an instant attraction, I'm afraid."

Emma blinked. "O—oh."

"I don't blame you." Gigi shrugged. "The boy has cheekbones that could cut glass, and he looks like one of those glorious angry fucks. You know, the ones who bottle it all up inside and then explode." She grinned. "I like the angry fucks."

"I'm not usually one for gossip." Emma chuckled. "But I wouldn't know if I know any in this instance. I can't tell you one way or the other."

"I just can't figure out why he did this to you. There were other options for getting rid of you, after all." Gigi shrugged.

The implication was clear.

Emma cringed.

Gigi continued after a pause. "I don't know what you did to make him so angry that he decided to torture you like this. He knows how important knowledge is, how we're all just creatures of context. He knew exactly what he was doing to you." She tucked a strand of Emma's hair behind her ear, still damp as it was. "He wanted to hurt you. Badly. And I expect now that you're back, he'll come to finish the deed."

"What do I do?" Emma fidgeted with the hem of her dress. "I couldn't stay in that house and walk its halls like I was already dead. Something was calling me here, something I can't explain. The Bishop's exorcism—I don't think it worked."

"I don't think it did either." Gigi sighed and draped her arm over Emma's shoulder. "I will tell you this much, strawberry. You didn't deserve a single lick of this—getting stuck in the middle when you were only trying to find your damn idiot brother. Here's what we do, at least in the short term. We'll close out the night here. I'll take you to my home, where you'll be safe, and we'll come up with a plan on how to deal with Raphael and the Mirror. I want you to get your brain back into that pretty head of yours, and then I'll put you on the next boat straight out of Arnsmouth. And you'll never look back."

"How do we get my brain back in my head?" She had to smirk at the description.

"Oh, I have no fucking clue." Gigi laughed. "Hence the bit where we come up with a plan."

Emma found herself smiling more than she had in six months. Even when there was talk of murder and vengeful cultists. Sitting next to Gigi made her feel more alive in that moment than she had since…well, whatever had happened to her.

There was hope. Hope that maybe, just maybe, she might have a path out of the darkness.

The door to the room burst open. Mykel stormed in. His expression for the first time was something that wasn't sinful and hungry teasing. Instead, it was a look of anger and panic. "Lady G. We have a problem."

Gigi sighed and stood from the sofa, smoothing out her dress and taking the time to flick one of her golden curls back. "The professor?"

"Worse." Mykel grimaced. "The Bishop."

Gigi had one word. *"Fuck."*

Mykel kept talking. "And he's asking for Emma."

Now it was Emma's turn. *"Fuck."*

CHAPTER TWO

Bishop Patrick Caner stood in the interior entrance to the jazz club and wrinkled his nose. It smelled and sounded like sin incarnate inside. Sex, drugs, and alcohol. None of that was his concern. Nor was it what he was reacting to.

There was dark magic at work in this place. The entirety of it was corrupted and felt like rotted floorboards creaking beneath his feet with each step he took deeper inside. It made his skin crawl, like ants were covering him. He did his best not to glower at every single person who looked at him with wide, nervous eyes. They weren't why he was in a bad mood.

He didn't care about the people who were quickly hiding their drinks, or the men and women pretending not to be holding hands with their lovers of the same sex. They weren't why he was here, either. He was here for one simple reason—he'd watched Emma walk in the door.

Emma *fuckin'* Mather.

And now he was here to throw her over his shoulder or drag her away if he had to. He cracked his neck loudly from one side to the other. The bouncer hadn't wanted to let him in—some chap named Connor—and Patrick had been forced to pop the man in the nose. Connor was having a good sit on the stoop outside with Patrick's handkerchief stuck to his bleeding face.

He disliked having to resort to physical violence. He really did.

Sadly, he was also really good at it.

This was the first time Patrick had come to the Flesh & Bone, despite knowing everything he needed to know about the establishment and the woman who ran it. He knew all about the Dark Society who called themselves "The Blade" and all the terrible and grotesque magic they performed on themselves and their initiates.

But sometimes it was better to let your enemies work out in the open than to drive them all into the underground. He could watch what he could see, and he could make sure the infection of Arnsmouth was kept…well, controlled.

Extermination was not always an option. Sometimes that only led to inviting in far larger and far worse insects. These ants were vicious, but they weren't as bad as what he knew would happen if he stomped them all out.

No, this infestation was to be managed. Kept in line. Didn't mean he had to like it. He sighed and tugged on his black cassock, straightening it. He knew he looked like a monolith on a good day. He certainly stood out amongst the crowd wearing their finest suits and dresses.

They were here to have fun. And they thought he was here to ruin it. He stepped under the beaded drapes, having to duck due to his height.

"My, *my,* aren't you just a walking wall of meat." A woman chuckled. "You're even bigger up close."

Patrick turned to see who had spoken and blinked. Standing there, leaning against the wall with all the casual confidence he could imagine anyone possessing, was…quite simply the most beautiful woman he had ever seen in his life.

She wore a clinging dress that hung on to every perfect curve, trailing down to the ground and pooling at her feet in ivory sequins. The dress was ivory and perfectly complimented her alabaster skin and pale golden hair. Her lips were curled in a devious and altogether unfriendly smile and were painted a flawless shade of crimson.

Patrick found himself staring exactly where he wasn't supposed to, but she was toying with a long string of pearls that drew his attention right to her cleavage. He hoped the warmth in his cheeks wasn't showing. "Um…"

"You must be the Bishop. I am Gigi Gage." She extended a hand to him, obviously inviting him to take it and kiss her fingers. "Welcome to my humble establishment."

Patrick shook his head, quickly remembering who she was and why he had come. "Emma Mather. Where is she?"

"Recovering in one of our private rooms. The poor thing is in quite the state." Gigi took a slow drag from her cigarette holder, and he caught himself once more staring at her, this time at those flawless red lips. She let out a long, lazy cloud of smoke, seemingly in no rush. "She's terrified, soaked to the bone, and came to a friend for help. What's so wrong about that?"

"She should not be here." He clenched a fist at his side. He wouldn't hit a woman. But Gigi was a monster, corrupted by the Great Beast, and one of the most dangerous people in the city of Arnsmouth. He had to remember that. "I've come to collect her and take her to the Church."

"Funny she didn't go there first." She hummed in mocking consideration. "She does know you, does remember you…but she came here instead, to someone she *doesn't* remember. Somehow, she knew that if she needed *real* help, she should come to me. Not some fancy light show and a pathetic attempt to purge what can't be cleansed." She gestured her cigarette at him dismissively. "You can shoo right along, Bishop. She isn't interested in talking to you."

"I will speak to her." He took a step toward the woman. He wasn't above using his height to intimidate. "No one here can stop me."

"Are you so certain?" She trailed her blue eyes slowly up and down his body, lingering at his waist. She chuckled. "It would be such a shame to waste a ham hock like you…what do you say? I propose this instead—come with me, let's have a fun night together, and you can forget all about Emma Mather."

He clenched his jaw. "No."

"I see how you're staring at me." She pushed away from the wall to walk up to him, trailing her hand over his chest to toy with the buttons of his cassock. "And as far as I know… the Church doesn't ban sex for their clergy. So, what's the problem?"

"I know what you are." He narrowed his eyes and thanked the Benevolent God that his cassock hid his body well enough to hide how his anatomy was reacting to even the notion of it. It was clear Gigi had designed herself to be exactly what she was proving to be—a seductress. "And I know what you're capable of."

"Good. Because I know what you are and what *you're* capable of." Her hand trailed lower, until it threatened to cup between his legs.

He snatched her wrist before she could, pulling her arm up over her head. "Enough. I don't want to hurt you, Gage. But I will."

She laughed, a sound like velvet and bells. She stepped into him, calling his bluff, and pressed her body to his. "Please make it hurt, Bishop. I'll be a good girl, I promise."

Patrick sighed and pushed her away, careful to not be too rough. He didn't want to cause a scene. "Stop, please."

"Damn." She snapped her fingers. "You found my weakness. The word *please*." She laughed coquettishly. "I am a sucker for when men beg me for things. Especially men in positions of power."

He ran a hand down over his face. He wanted to groan. This was not going at all how he expected it to, and he debated turning on his heel and fleeing. But he had come here for the poor girl, though he was starting to suspect they were both in over their heads. He dropped his hand heavily at his side. "Let's try this again."

"Oh, let's."

He fought the urge to scream. "Lady Gigi Gage, by the power of the Church of the Benevolent God, I am here to take Emma Mather into my custody. If you resist this act, you will be in violation of the Arnsmouth sanction of—"

"I know, I know." Gigi cut him off, making him swallow his words. He wasn't used to people cutting him off. He didn't know why that made his cheeks go warm. Before he could process what was happening, she was already sauntering away from him. She whistled like she was calling a dog and patted her thigh as she headed toward the back of the crowded room. "Come along, then, priest."

"I'm not a priest, I'm the Bishop." It was a foolish thing to complain about, but he didn't know what else to say as he followed the blonde through the room. He did his absolute best not to stare at her ass. But he knew that was very much what the dress was designed to make people do.

"No, you're a priest who they made Bishop. You have no right being where you are. You're just very good at…shining 'light' in 'dark' places. That's all." She didn't even glance over her shoulder while she spoke. "And that's all they need you to do. Has nothing to do with you being closer to your 'Benevolent' God."

He bristled at the insult and the sarcastic way she treated his faith. But what else was he to expect from her? She was a known member of the Blade, and if the rumors were correct, she may even be their leader.

Which made her both extremely deadly, and extremely useful. "What do you want with Emma?"

She shrugged. "At first? I wanted to keep her out of the hands of other people. Now? I just want to see the poor girl put back on her feet. That bastard did a number on her, and he needs to pay for what he's done." Gigi did turn to look at him that time, if only to glower at him. "And what you did."

"Me?" He arched an eyebrow. "What in the hells did I do? I was trying to save her."

"By what? Performing one of your little exorcisms?" She scoffed. "Please. You could have done much more harm than good trying to rip it out than if you had just left it there. Men. I swear, none of you can leave well enough alone."

It. What a way to describe the unknowable evil that plagued the city. It made the Great Beast sound diminutive. Harmless. Like nothing more than an ivy sprout climbing up a tree. But ivy could choke out even the strongest of oaks, given enough time.

And he knew firsthand what happened to those trees when they were felled by the creeping vines. It was his job to chop them down. The corruption left those infected by it hollow, empty, and brittle. A husk.

He refused to see that happen to Emma. "Losing her memories isn't nearly as bad as what would have happened otherwise," he muttered. The words were only half for Gigi as he assumed they would be swallowed up in the din of the club.

OF FLESH & BONE

Apparently not. Gigi stopped abruptly. He almost crashed into her, which would have been a very bad thing, considering their drastic size difference. She was his enemy, but that didn't mean he had any business accidentally flattening her.

She whirled to face him. "Men. Like I said! You"—she jabbed a finger into the middle of his chest—"are no better than that son of a bitch who took away her entire identity. Her life. The only thing she had left of her brother. You muck around with her because you feel that somehow you have the *right* to do it. And therefore, that somehow that makes you *righteous.*"

He wanted to argue with her. To tell her yes, he was being righteous, namely because he was, in fact, right. But he knew that it was like talking politics. There was sometimes simply no meeting in the middle. Gigi was a member of the Blade, and he was their sworn enemy.

He was only here for one single thing—fetch Emma Mather and drag her to safety. Not to get into arguments with the beautiful jazz singer.

But by the Benevolent God, she is beautiful, isn't she?
Damn it.

But she was. And he couldn't help but be reminded of it as she glared up at him. He smiled. It was kind of adorable. Like a very angry cat. Small, but bitey. And with very large claws, he suspected. A cat he knew better than to pick up by the scruff of the neck but one he didn't mind watching from a safe distance.

That seemed to only make her angrier. "That's all you have in response? You're going to just smile at me like an idiot?" In fact, his simple expression seemed to fluster her. It was the first crack in her armor that he had seen so far.

It only made his expression broader.

Gigi huffed in annoyance, turned on her heel again, and

stormed away. Patrick put his hands inside the pockets of his cassock and followed.

One mission.
Emma Mather.
Not Gigi Gage.
Not Gigi Gage.

"NOTHING SAYS CLASS LIKE TASSELS. *It's how you measure it, you know—class, that is. I bet there's a direct relationship to how elegant something is and the number of tassels attached.*"

Emma cringed at the voice of a young man speaking near her. A young man who very much wasn't there. But the voice felt familiar, even if she couldn't place it—like almost everything else in her life. Near but far, strange but known, family but stranger. She wondered if it was the voice of the brother everyone kept telling her she had.

She had heard a lot of voices in the past six months, things her father called echoes of the past—the sound of her memories playing out like a wax cylinder. Nothing to be afraid of. Nothing supernatural.

But it was damn unsettling, all the same.

She sat on a red velvet booth that ran the length of three walls of the small room, curving at the edges. The fourth wall was the way in and out, cordoned off from the rest of the club by thick tapestry-style curtains that were covered in, well, tassels. The same style of fabric draped the walls, hanging down low in swags and falls. She was playing with one of said dangly bits of string as she nervously sat on the booth in a stranger's clothes.

The Bishop was here. For her. She felt like she had been caught playing hooky and her father was here to shout at her. When Gigi threw the curtain aside with all the flair of a woman walking out onstage for their Broadway debut, Emma jolted in shock.

And behind her, ducking under the low doorway—low for him, anyway—was the Bishop. He looked ridiculously out of place in his stark, straight black priest's cassock that reached his ankles, and the severe cut of his otherwise all-black clothing. He found her and smiled with an expression that was at once both relieved and disappointed.

"Hello, Miss Mather."

"Bishop." She fought the urge to shrink away from him. She felt ashamed, though she wasn't sure why. She knew Gigi was involved in the Dark Societies. But neither Emma nor Gigi had done anything wrong. Yet.

That she knew of.

It was probably that last bit that was the problem, she suspected.

"Come. We're leaving." He reached out a hand to her. She was impressed at the size of it. "Let's take you to the Church, and we can sort through all this together."

"I..." Emma glanced between him and Gigi.

"I have answers I'm willing to give you for free, strawberry." Gigi sat down beside her, stretching out elegantly over the velvet cushions. "Because we're friends. Him? He's going to go mucking around in your head again. Just like that son of a bitch Saltonstall. Who knows what he'll rip out of you?"

"I'm trying to save you, Emma. I'm trying to help you. The path you're on leads only to rack and ruin. There is nothing but tragedy and darkness before you." Patrick shook his head. "Please. Please, come with me."

"I...believe you, but..." Emma didn't know what to do. Simply didn't know what to do at all.

"Some fates are worse than death." Gigi took a long drag from her cigarette. "And some deaths are waking ones that we have to suffer every moment we're alive. Trust me, strawberry." Gigi met her gaze, and Emma was shocked at the sincerity in her blue eyes. "I don't take charity cases often. But I want to help you. I want to get your memories back. He'll make sure they never, ever return."

She believed them both. And that was the problem. Neither of them was lying, but she didn't know which way to go. The Bishop was right that all the things that lurked in the shadows of Arnsmouth would guarantee she died a violent death. But what was her other choice? Living on like a ghost, this half-person, suffering a waking end every day she lived as her half-self?

"Your damnation is not limited to this world, Emma." Patrick took a step toward them but went no farther. He looked perfectly surreal against his extravagant surroundings. Like an apparition of faith. "You suffer now, but you will be rewarded for eternity. The opposite awaits you if you listen to Gage. You may solve your problems now, but your agony will last until the end of days."

"Oh, stop it with that pious nonsense." Gigi scoffed and dramatically rolled her eyes, draping an arm over Emma's shoulder as she did. "Behave now, or the Benevolent God will punish you for all eternity. Tell me—how is your god so Benevolent if he damns people to burn in the hells for all time? Hm? Doesn't sound very benign to me."

"Souls must pay for their transgressions. Especially those that they willfully commit."

"But don't you believe that the Benevolent God created all things? All of existence? So, it's his fault we're sinning in the first place." Gigi chuckled. "And don't give me that 'he's testing us' nonsense. He made us. He doesn't need to test us unless he's a sadistic bastard. And I have plenty of experience with sadism, *trust* me. Tell me, Patrick—do you?"

If Emma wasn't mistaken, she might have believed that the Bishop was blushing. Or he was furious. She couldn't really tell which. Could have been both. Emma shook her head. "I don't want to listen to a theological argument right now. I—I should go. I think it was a mistake to come to the city."

"Don't get scared off by his blather." Gigi stroked a hand over Emma's hair. "And besides…it's too late. The others already know you're here. I'm sure of it. And if they know, then they're already waiting in the wings to snatch you up. It isn't safe for you on the streets."

"Which is why she needs to come with me." The Bishop's tone suddenly left no room for argument. "Now."

Emma shrank away from the enormous man. "I…don't want to."

"But you don't want to stay here, either." Patrick sighed. "I don't want to hurt you, Emma. I want to help you. Let's go and talk things through, and I'll tell you all about the Dark Societies in the city and what they're after." He reached out to grab at her wrist. "Maybe once you understand what's truly at stake here, you'll—"

From down the front of her dress, Gigi produced a tiny, ivory-handled pistol from her cleavage. She pointed it straight at Patrick's head. "Touch her and you die."

Yes. Coming to the Flesh & Bone had been a mistake.

Patrick laughed. The kind of laugh that meant that he was very unimpressed with the gun. He straightened and cracked his neck. "That's how it'll be, eh?"

Coming to the Flesh & Bone was a very big mistake, indeed.

CHAPTER THREE

Emma had enough.
Standing, she snatched her purse from where she had put it on the coffee table in the crimson-colored velvet lounge. "No."

Gigi and Patrick were staring at her with matching expressions of confusion, as they were still locked in their very dramatic showdown. Gigi still had a gun pointed straight at Patrick, and Patrick had a—Emma didn't know. Magic. Maybe. Nothing she could see, but he didn't seem frightened in the slightest. She was sure he had some sort of trick up his sleeve.

She didn't care to find out.

"What?" Patrick blinked.

"No. Just no. I'm not doing this, I'm not going to watch this. I'm leaving"—she raised a hand to cut off both parties before they could speak—*"alone."*

Gigi stood, never taking the gun off the Bishop. "Emma, it's dangerous out there. Everyone will be out hunting you."

"Fine! Then let them. Maybe I should be dead. Maybe this is just my body catching up with the rest of me. But I'm not going to sit here and be stuck in the middle of whatever the *fuck* is going on!"

"I think it's far too late for that." Patrick sighed, his shoulders slumping. "At least let me escort you to—"

"No." Emma stormed from the little cordoned off velvet room, throwing the curtains aside angrily. She hesitated just on the other side of the barrier. "Thank you, Gigi."

The woman only laughed in reply.

Emma headed for the exit. She heard an argument continuing between the jazz singer and the Bishop, but she didn't hear gunfire, so she assumed it was mostly fine. She needed to get some air, even if it was still raining out, and she needed to get away from two sharks fighting over a hunk of raw meat.

Even if it meant there were five more sharks outside.

She felt alone, and small, and helpless. She felt so *weak.* She didn't know what was going on, she didn't remember a damn thing about herself, and all she had was the gun in her pocket.

"Seems like it's us against the world, eh?" The humidity in the jungle was intense. The man standing next to her was their guide, and he grinned at her with a cheeky roguishness that would have been annoying in a young man. But he was close to eighty, so it came off adorable.

The locals were not happy about the presence, and they were prepared to show it. With knives. And spears.

I'm insane. It isn't real. No one else reacted to the voices. No one else could see whatever the *fuck* that was play out. The things in her head were just harmless if disturbing.

At least the voices didn't make her feel so alone.

Mykel furrowed his brow and moved to stop her as she went for the exit of the club. "Kitten-baby, you shouldn't—"

With a snarl, she grabbed the man by the front of his expensive white suit and slammed him up against the wall.

He was twice her size, and she was absolutely certain the only reason he budged at all was because he hadn't been expecting her sudden wrath. "I swear if you *ever* call me that redundant shit again, I will *put a bullet in your balls.*" She glared up at him. "Do you understand me?"

"Y—yeah." He raised his hands in a show of submission. "Never again. Gotcha. I was just playing, Miss Mather. Just playing."

"Learn better manners." She shoved away from him and shook her head as she headed for the door. "And I know I'm about to die, and honestly? Right now? I don't care. Goodnight, Mykel. Thank the nice lady who loaned me her clothes."

"Sure thing, Miss Mather…sure thing."

She pushed open the door and hesitated again. She turned back to look at the man who was watching her with wide eyes. Not because she had shoved him but because he looked honestly worried. Now she felt bad, like she had kicked a puppy. "And you can just call me Emma. You know. If I live."

That made him smile, just faintly. "All right. Emma it is."

Emma turned and headed out into the night, her anger now a mix of confusion and desperation. She felt sick, like there were snakes in her stomach, and they were all very angry at her. She wanted to throw up. But at least the cold air helped.

Oh.

Shit.

Looking down, she sighed. She had no goddamn shoes. She had left her pair inside, soaked as they were, and now she was standing there on the brick sidewalk in nothing but her cotton stockings. At least it was early September, and it was still vaguely warm out.

Fine. Whatever. It didn't bother her. Something told her

this wasn't the first time she had wandered around places she shouldn't with no shoes on. It didn't hurt. She headed out into the night, her hand in her purse to keep a finger on the gun she carried. She didn't even know where she was going. To a hotel, probably. She had enough cash in her bag to pay for almost whatever she needed, and her father's name would get her anything else.

She began to walk through the city. It was two in the morning, and the streets were empty. Luckily, Arnsmouth was very small, and it wasn't a long walk from the West End where the Flesh & Bone was located down to the Plaza or to the Common where she knew there were a few decent hotels. She didn't want anywhere too fancy. Too fancy meant likely drama. No, she just needed a bed.

Pragmatism. That was what would get her out of the situation. Not panic, not fear, not desperation. Pragmatism. *Make a plan, Emma.*

Step One—get to a hotel. Get somewhere to sleep for the night. Ignore all the gossip that would come out of Emma Mather walking into a hotel wearing ill-fitting clothes and no shoes.

Step Two—wake up, go to a store, and buy clothes. And shoes.

Turning left, she decided to take a shortcut down an alley. It would take another ten minutes off her walk if she just darted between two rows of brick buildings. And her feet weren't sore, but they were soggy, and that was uncomfortable enough.

Step Three—get on the train home, because this had been an enormous mistake.

Step Four—

It was right as she was debating Step Four that she realized she could amend her decision to go down an alley to her list of mistakes. Not like she needed any more of them. She knew she was likely going to die after leaving the club, but she didn't think it'd be quite so immediate.

A hand clamped over her mouth. Her scream was muffled as someone dragged her against the wall. A knife was pressed to her throat, and she whimpered, bracing herself for the burning, stinging pain that would follow when the robber took her life.

Hopefully it was just a robber, and he was just going to kill her.

The other options were worse.

"Do not move. Do not scream. Do you understand me?" The voice that growled into her ear suddenly sent a shiver down her spine. Her whole body reacted to it, and not in the way she would have expected. Or wanted.

Instantly, her skin felt electric. The man who had her pressed against his chest smelled like sharp cologne, crisp and clean, with a hint of mint. Coupled with the danger of having his knife pressed to her throat, she felt heat pool low in her body.

Oh, this is a new discovery.

A very problematic new discovery.

In her distracted moment, the grip on her face tightened. The stranger repeated his demand. "Do you understand me?"

She let out a muffled "mm-hm" against his palm.

He released her face, only to wrap his arm around her and yank her firmly against his chest. "You are a fool, Emma Mather. A blind fool. What do you think you are doing?"

"I—do—do I know you?" She was shaking like a leaf. She held on to his arm with both hands but didn't dare pull on him. The knife at her throat ensured that she would keep perfectly still.

"Unfortunately." He sounded so angry.

"I'm sorry?"

"As am I."

Silence hung in the air for a moment before she broke the strange pause. "I assume you're Saltonstall?"

Her world whirled around as he slammed her against the brick wall hard enough that she saw stars. The knife was back to her throat, but now she could see his face—once she blinked away the spots, anyway.

Goodness. Gigi wasn't kidding. Those cheekbones *could* cut glass. If she and Saltonstall had been lovers, she suddenly understood why. Her errant and rather inappropriate thoughts were shoved away as the blade pressed harder to her throat, forcing her to tilt her head back. "Please, I—"

"Shut up." He glared down at her. His eyes were as dark as the night sky and were filled with such fury that she wished she could shrink away from him. But there was no escaping. He had one arm pressing against her chest, pinning her to the bricks.

Even if she tried to knee him in the crotch, he would likely stab her or slit her throat at the same moment.

So, she froze. And stayed obediently silent.

"You were warned. Again, and again, and again, you were warned. I told you a thousand times to stay away. To leave here, to save yourself. And yet like an *idiotic* moth, here you are." He pressed the blade harder to her throat. "I am here to put you out of all of our miseries."

She squeezed her eyes shut, waiting for it to happen. "Go ahead. You took half my life away. You might as well take the rest. I—"

More unexpected than being threatened and accosted in an alley was what happened next. With a knife against her throat, with her pinned to the wall, with the promise of imminent death...he kissed her.

And by all the powers that be, if he hadn't had her up against a solid surface, she would have collapsed. Her knees felt weak as he devoured her in that embrace. It was bruising and cruel—it was *starving*. He was kissing her in wanton need and overwhelming fury in the same exact moment.

She moaned against his lips. She couldn't help it. Her hands were grasping the lapels of his peacoat, holding on for dear life, as she let him overtake her like a wave. She wanted him to slide her up the wall and take her, right then and there. Or to throw her over a trash can and teach her how bad of a girl she really had been. She wanted to feel his wrath.

Yeah, I have very serious problems.

But she didn't care at the moment. All she could think about was how his tongue felt in her mouth as he deepened the embrace, a low growl leaving his chest as he pressed himself closer to her. She felt the extent of his desire pressed against her thigh.

When he finally broke away, she was breathless, her lips parted. But she wasn't left alone for long. The knife left her throat, only to trail up over her cheek, leaving goosebumps in its wake. She didn't dare move, no matter how hard she wanted to squirm.

"What am I to do with you?" He watched her from behind brass-rimmed glasses, still tracing the tip of the sharp knife over her skin in careful lines along her jaw and cheek. "You need to die. But…" Anger contorted his features again, but she suddenly realized it wasn't all pointed at her.

Oh, he was mad at her. Very mad at her. But he was also mad at himself. He knew he needed to kill her but couldn't bring himself to do it. At least not yet.

"We could—we could come to an understanding." She only dared to whisper when the knife wasn't near her lips. "A bargain. Y'know, quid pro quo, if you don't kill me."

He laughed, low and dark. "Emma, Emma, Emma…" He rested the point of the knife against her lower lip, dimpling the sensitive skin. He stared at it, his eyes lidded and pitch black with lust. A stray tendril of dark hair fell across his pale features, stirred loose from their kiss.

Emma wasn't so certain if she had ever been so turned on in her life. She imagined him forcing her to her knees, taking her with all that frustration, and anger, and lust. She imagined him pressing her face to the wall and bending her over, taking her like a street whore.

And she imagined him killing her.

She knew which options she preferred.

"I'm afraid not. As deeply tempting as you are." His expression cooled, and she knew which one it was going to be. Her stomach dropped.

I'm going to die now.

The knife left her cheek and she felt it against her throat again. She shut her eyes. "Just make it quick."

"I promised you it would be…though you don't remember, I suppose."

"Sounds like something I would make you do."

He chuckled and pressed a kiss to her cheek. "For what it's worth, I'm sorry. I do not want to do this."

"Thank you." She smiled faintly. "I guess that does mean something."

"Good—"

"Wait." She gripped his coat tighter. She didn't want to die. She really, really didn't want to die. Fear—real fear, the kind of knowing that what was coming next was inevitable and there would be no coming back. She let herself cry and didn't feel any shame in it.

"It won't hurt for long. I promise. This is a fairly painless way to die. Shock will set in quickly. I'll make sure to sever all your arteries at once. I am sorry, Emma." If she wasn't mistaken, his eyes were beginning to shine with his own tears. "I am so very sorry."

"Just—just tell me one thing."

There was a faint, sympathetic smile on him now. "Anything."

She sniffled. "Did we at least fuck once? And was it good? I suppose that's two things…"

He laughed quietly and leaned down to rest his forehead against hers. She could see a single tear slipping from the corner of his own eye. "Yes, Emma. On both counts."

"That's nice. At least there's that." Taking in a wavering breath, she held it and let it out in a long, shuddering sigh. "Okay. I'm ready."

He kissed her, and she knew he would hold the embrace as he did it. She let herself fall into the kiss, enjoying it, happy for the distraction. She needed it.

His hand tensed.

It was time.

A gunshot rang out.

CHAPTER FOUR

The first gunshot echoed so loudly in the narrow alley that it seemed to come from everywhere. Emma cringed and wished she could duck, but the knife at her throat kept her put.

The second gunshot glanced Saltonstall on the shoulder. He pulled back, placing his hand to the cut on his overcoat. But when he checked his palm, it seemed it hadn't hurt him.

"Third one goes in your head, professor."

Emma didn't care who was talking. She didn't care if it was a police officer, or if it was Patrick, or if it was the Benevolent God himself. Whoever it was had given her a chance to escape, and damn it if she wasn't going to take it. She ducked under Saltonstall's arm and made a break for the alley's exit.

"Emma!" He snatched at her, but she was too quick for him. She managed to dodge, even if it did send her staggering. Her hands touched the cold, damp bricks briefly as she struggled to keep upright.

When she straightened, she pulled up short.

What was a cowboy doing in Arnsmouth?

That was the first thought that hit her.

She stared at the man. She wasn't certain where or when she had seen a cowboy before, but she had the distinct impression that she had. And as she studied him closer, she corrected herself. Not a cowboy, a *gunslinger.*

The kind of man who thrived in the lawless days of the west. But he was too young to be part of that largely defunct group of people sent into retirement by the slow western creep of organized government. The man didn't look any older than she was.

The way he was glaring at Saltonstall told her of someone who was capable of being as ruthless as all the legends and stories she knew but didn't remember hearing. He was a few inches taller than she was and carried himself like a man twice his size. He was fairly thin, all things considered. His long, brown oilskin coat was pulled aside to show the holsters he had at both hips. One of the shining silver revolvers was in his hand, pointed at Saltonstall.

Beneath his wide-brimmed hat was dark hair that looked as though it had once been unevenly cut short but now was long enough to reveal it was rather curly. His beard looked as though it suffered the same fate. Once kept neat, and now left to run amok from mild negligence. Not once did he take his eyes off Saltonstall.

"Miss Emma, c'mere." The stranger held out his hand. "We're leaving."

"Who…are you?" She winced. She *hated* this game. "I'm sorry, I don't—"

"I know. It's fine. You don't know me. I'm Yuriel." Still, he didn't glance at her.

"Just Yuriel?" She blinked.

"Just Yuriel." He sniffed before his very serious expression creased in a lopsided, easy smile. "You're not the only one missing a full deck of cards, Miss."

Another victim of Saltonstall's, maybe? Emma wasn't sure. She knew she shouldn't trust the stranger, but if her options were either going with Yuriel or being killed by Raphael, she knew which one she would pick.

"We're leaving, professor." Yuriel's smile faded. "And you aren't following us."

"You don't understand what you're doing." The professor was keeping his distance, however. Emma watched the man in fascination as he stood there, his hair knocked loose from its swept-back styling. He was in the shadows of the buildings, now far out of the reach of the streetlights. He was all sharp angles and contrast, and it made him seem almost inhuman.

And if she wasn't mistaken, the darkness around him was…moving. She took a step closer to Yuriel. And a step closer to the light. *I had sex with him? And I lived? Shit.*

"I know exactly what I'm doing. Probably more than you do." Yuriel reached for her hand. She took it, not knowing what else to do.

"Emma. We can talk this through." Saltonstall was clearly trying very hard to sound welcoming and calm. It failed miserably and instead made his sinister demeanor much worse in the process. "I made a mistake. We can find a way around this. Come with me."

She laughed. She couldn't help it. "Sorry, bud. Hate to say that I don't believe you."

"Time to go, kid." Yuriel turned and headed down the alley, pulling her along for the first few steps. She walked beside him, and after the first ten or so feet, he let go of her hand. "We're gonna stay in the light. Got it?"

"Got it." Emma hugged herself to stay warm. She had no

coat, no shoes, and was wearing borrowed clothing. She didn't suppose she knew exactly how she was going to get the items back. But it was the least of her concerns at the moment. "Who are you?"

"Told you. Yuriel." The man glanced over his shoulder and let out a breath. "I hate that bastard. But at least he takes a hint." He released the hammer on his revolver and slipped it back into his holster. He pulled a hand-rolled cigarette from behind his ear and tucked it between his lips before fetching a heavy brass lighter from his pocket. "You want one?"

"No, I'm fine, thanks. I don't smoke." She studied him curiously. Maybe he was one of those people who just looked twenty, even though they were forty. It was hard to tell, as most of his face was obscured by his beard and hat. When she could finally see him in the light, and he looked at her, she pulled in a hiss of surprise. "Oh—"

One of his eyes was silver. And the other was gold. They shone like the brightest and most polished disks of the substance. It was decidedly unnatural.

Decidedly inhuman.

"Yeah." Yuriel chuckled. "It's fine. I don't got a beef with you, kid. But your instincts are right, I ain't what I seem." He puffed from the cigarette and let the smoke curl out of his nose. "I'm not gonna hurt you."

"Seems like everybody wants to do that, though. Or everybody's thought about it at some point or another." She glanced behind them, unable to help it. What was wrong with Saltonstall? Why did the darkness seem to writhe near him? And why did he want her dead? "I don't know why I'm so damn important."

He laughed, and when he talked, his cigarette bobbed up and down. "You are and you aren't. It's complicated. We'll talk about it more when we're somewhere—shit, why don't you have any shoes?"

It was her turn to laugh. He sounded so dismayed by the idea that she was walking around barefoot. "It's fine. I think I've walked barefoot for a long time on worse than bricks." She paused. "Though I couldn't tell you when or where."

"I know how that feels. The itch in the back of your skull that you just can't scratch. Like it's there, behind a door, and no matter how hard you smash into it, it doesn't budge. And for the life of you, you can't remember where the *fuck* you left the key." He sighed.

"Yeah. That's exactly what it's like." She frowned. "Did he take your memories, too?"

"Nah. My problem is entirely separate from what that asshole Saltonstall did to you." Yuriel bent his head to one side and then the other, cracking the bones loudly. He grunted. "A body this young has no right to be so sore all the time."

An odd statement, but fine. He was an odd man. Who was very likely not human. "What are you?"

"A better question than 'who.'" He sniffed then took another drag from his cigarette. "That's the bit I don't remember, kid. I don't know what I am. And I think I'm here to figure it out."

"Oh." She wasn't sure what to do with that.

"I'll explain more when we're out of the cold, and you stop shivering like an abandoned kitten." He narrowed an eye thoughtfully. "Is this the point I'm supposed to give you my coat? Is that the right thing to do here?"

She laughed again. "No, it's fine. I think that thing probably weighs more than me, anyway. I'd get flattened."

"Fair." He flicked some of the ashes from his cigarette onto the street. "We aren't going far."

"Where *are* we going?"

He glanced behind him again, ensuring that they weren't

being followed, before he replied. "I have a friend who has a place at the Docks. We'll be safe there."

The Docks weren't exactly a safe place to be on a good day, let alone at two in the morning. "You...sure? You aren't taking me there to, I don't know." She glanced behind herself again. "Do something worse, are you?"

He snorted. "Nah. You aren't my type, and I owe an old friend a big favor to keep you safe."

"Who?"

He paused thoughtfully for a second, debating answering her. He shrugged, as if deciding there was no harm in it. "Your brother. He told me to keep an eye on you. To keep you out of trouble. And that you'd come looking for him and end up in a right mess. And here you are."

"My—my brother? Do you know where he is?" How she wished she could remember him. She shook her head. "And I don't think this is all his fault. I'm sure I walked into this nonsense knowing exactly how dangerous it was."

"You did." He snorted in laughter. "You really did. And as to where he is?" He frowned. "I hate to be the bearer of bad news, kid."

"He's dead." She cringed. "Isn't he?"

"Yeah. He died at least a month or two before you arrived the first time. Before Saltonstall took your memories." He paused. "I'm sorry."

Her shoulders drooped. The news hurt. It felt like a knife in her gut, and though she couldn't remember her brother past the sound of his voice that she would hear in her hallucinated memories, something in her still felt his loss. "It's all for nothing, then. I got into this mess, lost my memories, and now I'm going to die, and it was all for nothing."

"Kinda."

She glared at him.

"What?" He lifted his hands as if in a show of surrender. "You said it, not me."

Sighing heavily, she ran a hand over her face. "I'm not leaving until I know what's going on. And not until I have my memories back or I'm dead."

"I figured. That's why I'm here. I hoped you'd get run out of town, and then I hoped you'd stay gone. Seems like you're stubborn, just like Elliot. Just in a different way." He placed a hand on her shoulder.

"How so?"

"He wouldn't ever get out of his own way. And you won't ever let yourself catch up." He chuckled. "You run a mile a minute, girl."

"Maybe I used to." She shook her head. "Not anymore." The streets were starting to turn craggy, the bricks placed much less carefully as they approached Arnsmouth Dockyard. The air smelled just a little worse in this area of town. Somehow musty, even though they were outside. *The tinge of fish and raw whale oil doesn't help.*

"Yeah. I suppose we'll have to fix that problem, won't we?"

"Which problem?" She was pretty certain he couldn't read minds and wasn't talking about the fish.

"Your memories. I know how you can get them back. I just don't know *how* you get them back." He wrinkled his nose. "That made a lot more sense in my head before I said it. You know what I mean."

"No, I don't think I do." She chuckled. She liked Yuriel, all things considered. Even if he did seem to have a problem with putting his foot in his mouth. It was weirdly endearing. Then again, she was pretty sure she'd find herself endeared to a sewer rat if it was nice to her at this point.

"I mean I know what you gotta do, I just don't know how we're gonna get you to do it. Easier said than done, and all that shit." He grumbled and flicked his spent cigarette away.

"I don't think English is my first language. Just can't remember what my original language *is*."

"I assume the way I get my mind back isn't the same way you get yours?"

"Nope." He smirked. "Wish it were that easy."

"You just said it wasn't going to be easy to get my memories back." They were approaching the back door of a large brick warehouse. The grimy windows were dark and hazy from likely never being cleaned once in their entire existence. Many of them were cracked, and some slots were missing entirely. Not a single light shone from inside. *Arnsmouth Ropeworks, Est. 1781* was painted along the side of the building in faded and flaked white paint.

"Yeah." He walked up to a wooden door and knocked once on the surface. It clicked and slid open, though Emma couldn't see anyone inside. "Getting your head back is going to be nearly impossible. But me?" He walked into the pitch-black building, leaving her standing on the sidewalk, watching. "For me, it's a death sentence."

She fidgeted, not sure if she should walk into the darkness after a definitely inhuman man she had just met. A man who claimed to have known her brother, but how was she supposed to know if that was true?

If she stayed outside, Gigi, the Bishop, or Saltonstall were going to find her. At least one of those three wanted her dead, but chances were it was at least two of them. She just didn't know which two. Hells, it could be all three, by her luck.

And only the Benevolent God knew what Yuriel was planning to do with her, if he wasn't telling her the truth. She covered her eyes with her palms and groaned. "I hate this. I just simply *fucking* hate this."

"C'mon, kid," Yuriel called from inside.

"Yeah, yeah." She threw up her hands as if to say she gave

up and walked into the darkness after him. "I'm coming, I'm coming."

Stay outside and almost certainly die.

Go inside and only probably die.

It was just one more roll of the dice.

CHAPTER FIVE

The wood floor beneath Emma's feet was splintery and rough, but at least it was dry. Not that her soaked stockings made that much better than it was before, but any improvement was worth celebrating. She was kind of having a rough night.

The ropeworks building they had entered was clearly not where the rope itself was made—that was a much longer, single-story building that stretched out along the wharf. This must have been where the finished lengths were coiled and readied for shipping.

Not that it really mattered. And not that Yuriel seemed to care anything about where they were. He just walked along ahead of her, hands shoved in the pockets of his oilskin coat as if he were walking through a park. He glanced at her over his shoulder. "C'mon, kid. Little bit farther to go."

"Where're you taking me?" She followed him. It wasn't like it really mattered, same as her surroundings. She had lost control over her life. All she could do now was to pick exactly how she was going to die. Well, not how. Except for Saltonstall, she didn't know the how—but maybe she could pick the who. The Bishop, the jazz singer, the professor...and now Yuriel. Every single one of them probably wanted to end her life. Saltonstall was just more honest about his intentions than the others.

"Downstairs. There're tunnels that'll take us to where we'll be safe. Out of their...eh...line of sight." He rubbed the back of his sleeve over his nose. "Mostly."

"None of that makes any sense, but sure." She shook her head. "And joy, more walking."

He chuckled. "Promise it isn't far." He went up to a door that went back outdoors. Furrowing her brow, she watched as he placed a hand in the center of the wood panel. After a pause, the door clicked, and he opened it.

Suddenly, the door was leading down to a flight of stairs that had no business being there. She peered out the window, and sure enough, there should have just been a walkway on the other side. Not stairs leading down into the darkness. "What the..."

"Magic." He smiled at her like she was eight and had just done the most adorable thing in the world.

"Right. Because that explains everything and is a perfectly normal response. Thanks." She glared at him halfheartedly.

"The members of the Key are an elusive pack, but when they do come out, they like to leave us little trinkets like this." He smiled and jerked his head down the stairs and began walking ahead of her. "They're bizarre. Never met one myself, but apparently they're on the friendlier side of things. For murderers."

"The Key?" She closed the door behind her. The stairway had flickering candles in sconces every fifteen feet or so. She wondered who kept them lit and maintained them. *Magic.* She rolled her eyes at her own idiocy. She'd catch up eventually.

"There are five societies that rule the city. You've met two of them tonight." He paused. "Three, I guess, if you count me. But I wouldn't."

"Oh?"

"Long story. Best told over alcohol. We'll get there." He shook his head. "Best to start at the top. The five Societies are the Mirror, the Blade, the Candle, the Idol, and the Key. Gigi is a member of—fuck, she's the *leader* of—the Blade. And the bastard with the knife is a member of the Mirror. Don't know if he runs it because I don't think anybody runs the Mirror. Bunch of elitist assholes, staring at darkness and pulling shit out of it they shouldn't know." Yuriel grunted.

"Why do the cults—sorry, Societ—"

"Nah, you had it right on the first count."

She smiled. Yuriel clearly didn't think much of the Dark Societies. She wasn't sure if that should make him more likable, but it did all the same. "Why are they split up? Don't they all worship the Great Beast?"

There was a large part of her that still didn't want to take any of it seriously—black magic, secret societies, and a demon that infested the city of Arnsmouth. It all sounded ridiculous. But she had seen just an inkling of its influence. Her father still refused to speak of what had happened during her exorcism and went pale every time she pressed him for details. Something had happened, something that wasn't natural. Something that went beyond the reach of what she could explain away as her hallucinations.

"They do, but they access its power in different ways. They all disagree about which way is the right way. The Beast has power over every aspect of human nature. Trying to control it directly would be like trying to hold back the tide with a teacup." He snorted. "It'd rip the person apart, so the *cults* just go after aspects instead. And regularly kill each other over it."

She had to admit that the topic, even though it was definitely going to wind up being the reason she died, was extremely fascinating.

As they reached the bottom of the stairs, she peered around Yuriel to see down the path ahead. The long, narrow brick tunnel was surprisingly dry for being underground near the harbor. To her relief, the ground was hard, packed dirt. It was dry, and more importantly, it was smooth. She didn't think she could handle any more uneven bricks or splinters. The corridor was narrow enough that she couldn't see very far around Yuriel. The flicking of the light against the brick arch overhead provided most of what she knew about where they were going. And it wasn't much. He could be leading her to the hells themselves and she wouldn't know the difference.

He scooped up a candle from one of the sconces and held it in front of him as he walked, casting flickering shadows along the brick walls around him. Wrapping her arms around herself, she frowned. "I think I saw things in the professor's shadows."

"You did. He's corrupted. Those *things* you saw eat whatever they touch. Stay in the light if you're around him."

"I don't think being around him is a smart idea, period."

"You're right. It isn't."

"But…what is he?"

"He's still human, even if he should've been destroyed by the darkness a long time ago. He's figured out some way to keep it at bay, though I don't know how." Yuriel shrugged idly. "Doesn't matter. Like any dam, it'll wear out. Water goes where it wants to go, it just takes time. And it's patient. Very patient. The Great Beast will have him soon enough."

"I suppose if you're that big and that old, you would have to be patient." They walked in silence for probably another moment before she couldn't help it. She had so many questions. "So…what are you?"

He glanced back at her briefly before letting out a long, dreary sigh. "I don't know. That's the trouble."

"You don't know?"

"I don't remember."

She didn't know what to say for a long moment, except the obvious. "I know what that's like. I'm sorry."

"It's all right. I'm starting to wonder if some things are better off not being known. But missing your entire identity is something else entirely." He huffed a single laugh. "I guess you really would understand, wouldn't you?"

"I keep being shown photos of myself. Being told stories about myself. Things that I can't deny probably happened—but that are as empty for me as anything else. It's the life of a stranger but someone I desperately wish I knew." She wasn't sure why she was telling him all this. Yuriel could be lying to her. Somehow, she didn't think he was. "You don't know anything at all?"

"Oh, I do. But I don't want to scare you off."

Why did that sound like a challenge? "I don't scare easily."

"I don't think you can handle it." Now she knew he was goading her.

She nudged him in the back. "Come on."

"No."

She shoved him, not that it budged him in the slightest. He was a lot heavier than he looked. "Tell me!"

He laughed. "When we get where we're going."

"Which is when, exactly?" She really was sick of walking. Exhaustion was starting to set in. She was cold, wearing someone else's clothes, still damp, just had her life threatened, nearly died, and now walked halfway across the city barefoot. She needed a drink and some damn sleep.

"Right about now." Yuriel stopped and turned to face the brick wall before placing his palm against the rough surface.

It shimmered and disappeared, revealing another offshoot from the main corridor.

This could all be a dream. But it was hard to argue with disappearing walls. "Huh," was the best she could come up with at the moment.

He smiled at her and shrugged. "You get used to it."

"I suppose." She glanced back down the way they had come. "How many doors did we pass without knowing it?"

"Who knows?" He stepped into the newly-appeared hallway. "I don't have the key to those."

Keys and doors and corridors that shouldn't exist. Things that infested people. Dark Societies and Great Beasts. "I need alcohol."

He cracked up at that, shaking his head. He took off his wide-brimmed hat to run a hand over his dark hair, ruffling the curls that looked a little unruly at best. She could sympathize, as her hair was prone to doing the same nonsense. "I can help with that."

She followed into what seemed to be a large, old storeroom. It was mostly empty save for a few crates here and there and some boxes of what looked like supplies. A table and two chairs sat by one wall, and a bedroll was laid out by another. More candles were burning in sconces, lighting the room in flickering shades of amber.

It was also as silent as a tomb. Something she tried very hard not to think too much about.

Yuriel walked over to the table and tossed his hat onto the wood surface, not caring about the few bottlecaps and playing cards that scattered as it landed. He shrugged out of his oilskin coat next, tossing it over the back of the chair. He was surprisingly skinny, and her suspicion that he carried himself like a bigger man was confirmed. He sank down into the chair with a groan, then gestured idly to the seat across from him.

Just happy at the idea of being off her feet, she sat. It was precisely when she stopped moving that it all hit her at once. The reality of it. She let out a long sigh.

With a knowing chuckle, Yuriel plucked a bottle off the ground by the wall and uncorked it before handing it over to her.

She did sniff it before she drank it, mostly out of curiosity for what she was about to put in her face and not because she had any intention of *not* having any. Moonshine whiskey. She took a sip, coughed, and took a second.

Yuriel was still smiling at her as he leaned back in his chair. He took one of his two guns from his holsters and placed it down—facing away from her, thoughtfully—before he began to dismantle it.

"So...what are you?" She took another sip of the moonshine. It was rough, but she suspected she had drunk far worse in her life with how little it bothered her.

He watched her for a second with those strange silver-and-gold eyes and then sighed. "I have two options. I am either an angel...or a demon. And I don't know which."

She blinked. Went to speak, stopped, shut her mouth, tried again, failed again, and with a snort of a laugh, took a swig from the alcohol. "Well. Shit."

His shoulders relaxed as if he had been worried about how she was going to respond. Scratching idly at his beard, he looked away toward the entrance of the chamber. They could see out through the gap, but she wondered if anyone could see *in.* She hoped not. She didn't want to know who else—or what else—called the tunnels home. After the long pause, Yuriel spoke again. "I'm here to do either good or evil. And I don't remember which."

"You think they would have pinned a note to your shirt on the way out the door."

That made him laugh. He reached down by the wall and

produced his own bottle of liquor. Raising her bottle to his in a toast, they tapped them together with a quiet *tink* before going back to quietly drinking for a moment.

An angel or a demon. Good or evil. She hummed thoughtfully. "How do you find out if you're an angel sent here for good, or…?"

"See, that's the thing." He leaned forward, resting his arms on the table. "It's reversed. I'm either an angel *trying* to fall, or a demon *trying* to ascend. In short, I'm fucked. I don't know what I'm supposed to be doing, but here I am. With vague memories of the Civil War, the Wild West, and a promise to your brother that I intend on keeping."

That sounded like a headache. Suddenly, her own memory issues didn't seem nearly as big of a deal. "Why?"

He raised an eyebrow. "Why what?"

"Why keep the promise? Unless you're a demon trying to do right."

"Your brother helped me. It was one of the last things he did. I owe him a favor, and as far as I know, my kind keeps their promises regardless of where they're from." He cracked his neck loudly before taking a sip of the hard alcohol. "One way or another."

"I guess. I don't know anything about what angels and demons are really like. Just the myths they teach in the books. I expect that has no basis in reality."

"Your guess is as good as mine, kid." He snorted. "Not only didn't I get sent with a note pinned to my damn chest, I didn't get a manual, either."

She twisted in the chair to lean against the wall and started rubbing her foot, taking some time to think it all through. And drink. Mostly drink, honestly. "Now what do we do?"

Yuriel took a rag from the table and began cleaning the parts of his gun one by one. He let the silence hang in the air for a long moment before he answered her. "We go get your memories."

"And how do we do that?"

"The Dark Society of the Mirror owns a relic. A powerful thing that lets you see inside your own mind and can show you what's in the minds of others. The professor has it hidden away somewhere inside his house. You and I are going to go find that mirror." He peered down the barrel of his gun and then blew through it, clearing some fleck of something from inside. "And we use it to get your head back on straight."

"And how, exactly, are we going to get in and find the mirror?" She didn't expect Saltonstall was going to just let them borrow it for an hour.

"Well…" He smirked. "I expect we're going to have to shoot the bastard." His expression went cold. "Is that something you're prepared to do? Kill somebody? It might come to that, Emma. This is the road you're walking down."

"Barefoot," she muttered. But that wasn't the reason her own mood had suddenly darkened. Could she kill someone? Maybe she already had, and she didn't remember. But she felt like that was something that never left a person, no matter how far removed they were from who they once were. Or maybe she simply hoped that was the case.

"Can you kill Professor Saltonstall?" he asked again.

"He tried to kill me." Now she was pouting, and she couldn't care less about it.

"Not talking about self-defense. I'm asking if you could take this gun of mine, point it square in his defenseless face, and pull the trigger. Because if you can't—there ain't no point in trying to do this. We'll get you on a train home, and that's that." He was watching her now, those weird silver-gold eyes of his boring into her.

She stared down at her sore foot instead of meeting his

gaze. "Something in me won't let it be over. I can't go back to that house, walking around like a ghost—like a shell of a person."

"But can you do what you'll need to do to fix it?"

Could she?

Could she honestly kill someone in cold blood?

Shutting her eyes, she sighed. "I don't know."

"Good."

Looking up in surprise, she found him smiling. He casually returned to cleaning his gun. She stammered for a moment before finally getting out, "Excuse me?"

"If you said 'yes,' I'd know you were lying. If you said no, that means you'd be back on a train to go off and live however long you wanted before you probably wound up killing yourself to make it stop." He sniffed. "Nobody knows if they can murder until they've been given the opportunity. And anybody who tells you otherwise is full of shit."

"I...suppose." She stared off thoughtfully. "So..."

"So, you get some rest while I get you some proper clothes and get us both some supplies. We break into his home, maybe murder the bastard, and find that fuckin' mirror. Simple."

"Simple." Right. Sleep did sound good.

He jerked his head toward the bedroll. "Hope you don't mind. I promise I don't have fleas."

She smiled. "I feel like I've slept on a lot worse."

"I knew I'd like you." He pushed up from the table, pulled his coat back on, and picked up his hat. "There's a knife on the box over there, and you've got your gun. Sleep with both next to you. Just in case." And with that, he took a left out of the room and down into the tunnel, and...she was alone.

And that made everything so much more frightening. She headed over to the bedroll with her purse, scooping up the knife as she passed it, and lay down on the pile of blankets and meager padding. She meant what she had said—she was pretty damn certain she had slept in a field with nothing underneath her before.

But the context had likely been very, very different. Shuffling so her back was to the wall, she tucked her small gun under the rolled-up blanket she would have for a pillow and held the knife close to her chest. Shutting her eyes, she tried her best to sleep. But every few seconds she would open them to look at the opening out into the hallway.

Everything was perfectly silent to the point she could hear her own heartbeat. And it was going far faster than she'd like. Shutting her eyes again, she tried to focus on breathing slowly.

"In caves, the mind can play tricks on you. It tries to see things where nothing exists, hear things where there isn't any noise." The voice of her father sounded like he was right there next to her. But she knew better. Especially when her own voice answered.

"I hear voices on a good day, Poppa. It won't bother me."

Poppa. She called her father Poppa. That made her smile. Just a little piece of herself was back. And hopefully she'd soon have the rest.

And hopefully she wouldn't have to kill Saltonstall to do it.

Hopefully.

But something told her she wasn't that lucky.

CHAPTER SIX

Patrick was in a *mood.*

"Do you see what you've done?" Gigi shoved him with both hands as she shouted up at him. "Now she's as good as dead!"

It wasn't like she could push him an inch, but to make her feel a bit better—or at least calm her down—he took a step back anyway. "I wasn't the one who sent her away."

"You barged in here. I had her. I was going to keep her safe."

He snorted. "Safe. Sure. The kind of 'safe' that you people practice is the kind that puts people in shallow graves." He grimaced. "Or worse. Sometimes they get put there and don't stay there." *Benevolent God, I hate the Candle. They give me the willies.*

She laughed. "You have no idea what you're speaking about, *Bishop.*" She said his title with such disgust he half expected her to spit on the ground at his feet. But it seemed she was too much of a lady for that. "Get out of my establishment."

"I'm leaving. Not because you asked." He stepped back up

to her, towering over her, using his height to his advantage. He didn't like resorting to it, but damn if it didn't come in handy. "But because someone has to go save her."

"You can't help her." Gigi sneered up at him, apparently entirely unaffected by his attempt to intimidate her. She placed a hand on his chest, and he froze as she slid her fingers beneath the buttons of his cassock. Her voice lowered, her anger turning into something that was both sultry and full of disdain. "There's only one person who can help her, and he's going to kill her. Before you stormed in here, I was going to help her negotiate with the professor. Now I'm simply left to wonder whether he'll fuck her before or *after* he slits her pretty little throat."

Taking Gigi's wrist, he pulled her hand out from his clothing. She was a dangerous snake. Beautiful, flashy, venomous, and insidious. She could kill him before he even noticed the fangs. "What do you want with the girl?"

"Me?" Gigi huffed and yanked her hand out of his wrist. "I want to see her fixed and out of here. I want to see her kept out of the grasp of people who would use her for their own ends."

"Bullshit."

"Don't believe me. I don't care." She turned on her heel and stormed away from him, disappearing back into the velvet-shrouded alcove of the floor.

Was he supposed to follow her?

Or was he supposed to leave?

Nobody had just exited a conversation like that with him in…he couldn't remember. Ever? He wasn't used to being brushed off. He wasn't sure what to do.

Gigi pulled back the curtain and glared at him. "Get in here, you enormous idiot." The angry drag of the copper rings of the curtain punctuated the end of her sentence as she veritably slammed the proverbial door in his face.

He sighed. Brushing the curtains aside, he ducked back into the room, half expecting to have a dagger shoved into his ribs the moment he did. But no. Gigi was sprawled back out on the cushions, looking entirely resplendent. Her frustrated expression and the way she was glowering at him made her, annoyingly and counterintuitively, more appealing.

She lit a cigarette and took a drag off it, leaving him standing there waiting for her to speak. He simply folded his arms across his chest. He wouldn't play her game. He wouldn't. So, he waited.

Finally, she lifted a shoulder in an indifferent shrug and gestured to one of the chairs. "Sit. You take up too much space."

That made him chuckle, though he was sure it was meant to be an insult. "My mother fed me right." He sat down in the chair near the curtained exit. Not that he wasn't in a dangerous situation. He couldn't see whoever, or whatever, might be lurking on the other side.

"Apparently." Gigi took another long, slow pull from her cigarette. "You and I want the same thing right now, ham hock. We want the girl safely out of Arnsmouth, and safely out of the reach of the people who would use her like they did her brother."

He snorted. "If you're suggesting we work together—"

"Oh, don't start with your self-righteous, overbearing, zealous bullshit." She rolled her eyes. "I am going to say this once and only once, priest. Your religion is not, nor shall it ever be, the answer to everything."

"Don't begin to pretend that this is simply a theological debate between us, Gage." He tightened his hand into a fist. "You are a murderer. Your *friends* are all murderers. What you practice is not a religion, it's a perversion. Your—"

"What I practice is freedom." She slammed her cigarette

case down on the coffee table between them. "What I practice is what lets me live a life out from under the thumb of all those who would control me, use me, and climb on my corpse for their own profit and amusement. But you wouldn't understand that, now, would you?"

He stared at her silently for a moment. "No. I would not."

"Good. At least you aren't a total fool." She shook her head. "What we do is not for the sake of cruelty. You're talking to the wrong person for that. The people I hurt?" She sneered. "They beg me for it. But the people who get a thrill from murder and pain? Those are exactly who I'm trying to keep her away from."

"Now you want to pretend that you're somehow nobler than the others, simply because the people whose lives you ruin *ask* for it?"

"Yes." She crossed her legs as she sat back. He found that far more distracting than he should. "That is precisely what I'm 'pretending,' priest. There are two groups in this city we must keep her away from at all costs, and you know who they are. I'd rather she end up dead than with them. But what I am trying to do, whether or not you believe me, is to save her from herself. To get her memories back, and then put her on the next boat to Tibet if I have to."

"Why do you care?"

"I made the mistake of getting to know her, even just a little. I like her. Even more than I liked her brother." Gigi laughed, a sound that wasn't entirely friendly and more than a little sarcastic. "I have a problem with taking in strays."

"I see."

"I can't save her on my own. Neither can you. But we might be able to do something if we stop bickering about whose god is mightier. We can go back to loathing each other the moment she's either in the ground or overseas."

It was an interesting proposition and an even more interesting choice. Most of him railed at the idea of teaming up with the murderous cult leader—it would likely be more trouble than it was worth. But there was some sense in what she was saying. No one would expect him to work with Gage, even for the smallest amount of time.

"What will the rest of your *Society* think about your plan?" He wrinkled his nose.

"They can go fuck themselves." Gigi smirked. "My rule is law."

Ah. Gigi Gage *was* the leader of the Blade. That made the idea even more interesting. It might give him the opportunity to see into the workings of the Blade, and if he was lucky? Maybe he could stop them entirely. If he could get Gage to trust him even just a little…he might be able to snap the neck of the viper before it turned on him.

She was likely thinking precisely the same thing. That if the snake got the wolf to trust her, she might have the opportunity to sink her fangs into his neck when his guard was down.

But it was a risk he would take if it meant rooting out the entire snake den in the process. He leaned over and stretched his hand out to her. "Fine."

With a thin, knowing smile, she placed her hand in his. "Let's get started, then."

They hated each other.

They were likely going to kill each other.

But for now?

They were going to work together.

EMMA WOKE up with the distinct sensation that someone was watching her. Snatching her gun from underneath the pillow, she sat up. Her head reeled with the suddenness of going from flat and asleep to vertical and awake. But one thing very quickly became clear—she was right.

She wasn't alone.

Pressing her back against the brick wall, she clenched the gun tight and held it in front of her with both hands. "And who the *fuck* are you?"

The man laughed. He was maybe her age—barely over twenty, with short black hair and handsome, youthful features that sat in stark opposition to how simply vicious he looked. Something about him reeked of violence. "Easy, little girl. No need to get riled up." His accent sounded as though he was from India, though it had faded a bit. He was dressed in worn and faded clothing, the hem of his pantlegs threadbare. He looked, well, like a street urchin who had survived a few years longer than most.

He was sitting on one of the crates, one foot up on the box, his arm draped over his knee, the other leg idly swinging as he watched her with the amused grin of a sibling who had pulled off a successful prank.

More troubling was the small blade he had in his hand, flipping it around his fingers, back and forth and around, with all the skill of a man who had been doing it his entire life. She had no doubt he could throw it from where he was sitting and likely put it straight into her chest.

"Please answer my question." She didn't relax her grip on her gun, even if it felt pretty useless at the moment. "I'm having a really bad few months, and I've decided I have zero patience for games. And please, if it isn't an inconvenience, tell me upfront if you plan on killing me. I dislike finding this out later."

That made him cackle as if she was the funniest thing in the world. He leaned back against the wall, the smile never leaving him. "I'll start at the top. Name's Robert. Just a kid on the streets. And no. No plans on killing you right now. But in Arnsmouth, everything's subject to change."

"Fair." She slowly lowered her gun but kept it in her lap. "Next question, why are you here?"

"Few reasons." He kept flicking his own small blade around his fingers. "First, bringing you some supplies." He pointed with the blade at a carpet bag on the ground near him. "Clothes and the like. Second, I wanted to see what all the gods-damned fucking fuss was about. Here comes Emma Mather, and all the city's in a tizzy." He looked her over then shrugged. "Don't seem too special."

"Thanks." She ran a hand through her hair, trying to smooth it down. "I don't feel too special either, if that makes you feel any better."

"A bit." He flicked his knife around again, watching her with an expression that reminded her of a predator watching its prey. It was hungry, curious, and eager to see what her next move might be. "Little girl, lost in a big game."

"You're my age. Don't call me a little girl." She pushed up from the bedroll and grabbed the handles of the carpet bag, half expecting him to kill her at any moment. But he didn't stop her as she took it over to the table and started laying out its contents. Clothing that would fit her, shoes, and a set of lockpicking tools. *I guess we are going on a bit of a caper, aren't we?* "Where's Yuriel?"

"Out dealing with issues. Told me to bring you some shit, so here I am, bringing you some shit."

It was a risk turning her back on him. But she had the opinion—where she got it, she didn't remember—that showing a predator she wasn't afraid was the easiest way to get them to not see you as a potential victim.

It was probably wrong. It'd probably get her killed. But she kept her gun with her and set it on the table beside the carpet bag. "How much is he paying you?"

"A lot. And not in cash, either. I trade in favors, little girl. And favors are worth far more than gold."

"Don't call me that."

"Say please."

Oh. He was a sadist. That was charming. Turning to look at him, she leaned against the edge of the table and folded her arms across her chest. "If I say please, it's a gift, and if I don't, it's a favor?"

"You got it." He paused. "Little girl."

She rolled her eyes. "Please stop calling me that."

"Done! See, we're friends now."

"Right." She watched him for a moment. He seemed content to just be stared at and stare back for a few beats of silence. "So, which one are you with?"

"Excuse me?" He leaned his head back against the brick wall, looking as casual as could be. He wouldn't be so deeply unsettling if it weren't for the constant flicking of his blade between his fingers.

"Which cult?"

Robert laughed hard at that and shut his eyes. "It's not that simple. I just know people, and I get things done. Rich and poor, high and low, good and evil. Doesn't matter. I'm a broker, that's all."

"Sure." She shook her head. She wasn't sure she believed him, but she certainly wasn't going to argue. "Well, now what?"

"Hum?"

"Are you going to just sit there and stare at me for the next few hours, or do you have another point in being here?" She tilted her head to the side as she watched him, still a bit nervous to take her eyes off him for too long. "I'd like to change, and I'm sure not going to do it with you here."

"I see how it is. I show up, try to make friends, and you push me right back out the door." He huffed in false indignance. His grin told her that he didn't take her insult seriously. "Fine! I'll leave. Tell your new guardian *whichever* that I said hello."

Robert hopped off the box and headed toward the exit to the chamber. "Oh! One last thing. When you want real answers? And I mean *real* answers? Come to me. I can take you to Thaddeus."

"Thaddeus?" She shrugged, as if the first name meant something to her.

"If you don't know Doctor Thaddeus Kirkbride, you're lucky you come from money. Especially with your"—he tapped a finger to his forehead—"issues."

She might not have known him by his first name, but she knew Dr. Kirkbride. A chill went down her spine. He was the head doctor of Arnsmouth Asylum, and she knew—just *knew*—that she wanted to stay as far away from him as possible. "No. I don't want to talk to him."

"Shame. Because he really wants to talk to you, new girl."

"I suppose that's better than 'little,' but..." She shook her head. "No. I'm not going to go anywhere near him. Or that place."

"Not yet." He chuckled. "But you will. You very much will want to soon. And when you do? Come find me."

"How will I be able to find you?"

"Just look. I'll be there." And with that, he headed out the doorway and was gone. Emma was left alone. The silence took over like a wave.

Letting out a slow breath, she started changing into the new clothes. She was happy to have a set that fit her properly and was even more excited for the shoes. Examining the lockpick set, she turned it over in her hands. She knew what each piece was for. *I know how to pick locks, apparently. That's convenient.*

Monsters and murderers. She was well and truly over her head. But hey, she could pick a lock. Great.

She wasn't sure how long she stood there, debating the set of picks, when she heard someone approach. Grabbing her gun again, she whirled.

"Hey, easy, there." Yuriel lifted his hands in surrender. "Just me, kid. Just me." He eyed the bag. "I see you had a visitor. No wonder you're jumpy."

"Is Robert a friend of yours?"

"No. Just useful to know." He headed over to the table and began to reassemble his second revolver with impressive speed. It was clear he had practice. "We're going to do this now before Robert sells word of where we are and that I asked him to get you some lockpicks. He'll put the math together soon enough if he hasn't already."

It was time. Part of her was relieved. Part of her was terrified. Gathering her things, she tucked her gun and the lockpicks into her purse and slung it over her shoulder. "Breaking into the house of a man who is trying to kill you is nuts." She snickered. "Good thing I'm nuts."

He slung an arm around her shoulder and pulled her into a hug, and to her surprise, put a kiss against her temple. "I'll do what I can to keep you safe. But when it comes down to it, this is all up to you."

"Well, then, we're doomed."

"Yup." He patted her on the arm as he walked toward the exit. "Entirely doomed. C'mon."

"What time is it?"

"Almost dawn."

"We're going to break into his house in broad daylight?" She followed him, jogging the first few steps to catch up as he led her out of the tunnel in a different direction than the way they had come.

"Seems a good time to do it, seeing as the darkness around him is carnivorous."

She opened her mouth to argue, thought about it for a second, and promptly realized he was right. "Point."

"You might have to shoot him, Emma. You might have to kill him. And it might not be in self-defense."

"I...I know." She wrapped her arms around herself, glad for the coat that Robert had brought her. "I guess we'll know if I'm capable of it pretty soon."

"I guess so."

They fell into silence as they walked, with only their footfalls on the packed dirt floor to fill the air. Monsters and murderers. Now she was going to find out if she was one, herself.

Or if she'd be just another smear of blood on the pavement.

CHAPTER SEVEN

"This is an exceptionally bad idea." She couldn't help but complain as she knelt by the doorknob and stuck her pick into the keyhole. They were standing at the door to Saltonstall's walled garden. It wouldn't be too hard to pick, but that door only got them to the other side of the brick wall. Not inside the house.

"Definitely." Yuriel was standing guard. It was the early morning hours, so people were still in the process of getting up and going about their days. The back alley of the brownstone rows was narrow and quiet. The heavy vines that dotted the street helped obscure them. Kind of. It was fine. Everything was fine. This was all going to be *fine.*

That was what she kept telling herself.

A complete and total horseshit-dung-heap lie.

The lock clicked. She was honestly a little disappointed. As eager as she was to get off the street, it was one step closer to potentially having to deal with Saltonstall. Something itched in the back of her mind as she thought over their encounter. He had shed a tear at the idea of killing her. He had hesitated in slitting her throat.

What in the hells had passed between them? Why was she terrified but drawn to him? They had made love, that much was clear. So, there was an attraction. But was there anything else?

Would she live long enough to find out?

"C'mon, kid." Yuriel ducked inside the brick wall and shut the door behind them. He jerked his head toward the small back shed and pulled her behind him. "All right. So." He pulled his gun out of his holster. "Here's the plan. You get inside, and you find the mirror."

"What? That's your brilliant plan?" She kept her voice as much of a hiss as she could while still trying to shout at him. "Just go find it? I don't know where it is!"

"Sshhh!" He glared at her. "You've seen it before. You know where it is. You just don't remember."

"That's the same—" She let out a frustrated sigh as she lowered her voice at his frantic gesturing. "That's the same thing."

"It isn't. You *know* it." He poked her in the forehead. "It's in there somewhere. You have to trust yourself."

"Says the guy who can't remember if he's an angel or a demon." She narrowed her eyes at him and, reaching up, poked him in the forehead. "You have to just trust yourself."

He growled. "Yeah, okay. Fine. I'm feeding you bullshit. But it's the only shit we have to go on. If you don't find the mirror, I ain't gonna be the one to do it." Rubbing a hand over his face, he scratched his beard. "This is the plan—you're going to sneak in. I can't cat burgle worth shit. I sound like a team of horses pulling a wagon. I'm going to wait outside. You're going to look for the mirror. If Saltonstall wakes up, or sees you, you shout, shoot through the window or whatever, and I'll bust in and save you."

That was a bit better. Not by much, but at least a bit. Shutting her eyes for a moment, she took a breath and let it out slowly, steadying herself. Fine. She could do this. She nodded once to him.

"Good. Let's go." He ducked around the wall, leading the way to the back door. He kept close to the wall as he went in case Saltonstall was looking out his window. She ran close behind him, keeping herself ducked and low.

The back door was mostly glass with an old-fashioned lock. They didn't really have tumblers so much as they just had a series of posts she had to push. Easy. She knelt by the lock and grabbed the right tool from the kit Robert had given her.

"Hurry up."

"Don't rush me." She tried not to laugh at his impatience. She had only just started. Plucking the right pick out of the kit—which looked more like a hook than anything else, she put the tensioner in the lock and began her work. It only took her a few seconds before it clicked.

Gesturing with a jerk of his head, he encouraged her to go inside. But inside was danger, and danger was likely to get her killed. And more importantly, inside was alone. But it had to be done.

With another dreary sigh, she took off her shoes and carefully tucked them into her purse. They were pretty flat and comfortable, but they still made more sound than bare feet. Producing her pistol, she held it down at her side. She didn't want to shoot someone if she didn't have to, and she didn't want to get startled at the wrong moment and put a hole in Saltonstall's head only because he had snuck up on her.

The house was silent. She padded carefully down the hallway, peering around each corner as she went. Luckily, the house was moderately new, and the floorboards weren't too chatty.

Now what?

She was inside. Maybe they should go to the basement? *Basement seems like a really obvious place to store an evil mirror. That would be the first place the Investigators would look, so that's probably the last place it is.* She started climbing the staircase up to the second floor, careful with each step, and staying on the carpeted spots as much as possible.

If I were an evil professor who practiced dark magic and had a giant, evil, mind-sucking mirror, where would I put it? Attic is obvious. Basement is obvious. No...it's gotta be hidden through a secret door or something.

There was a library on the second floor, and something about it tugged on her. She knew she had been there before. Stepping in, she took in the rows of books and trinkets. The morning sun was cutting sharp, golden shapes on the wood floor and carpet, leaving her more than enough light to see.

Something flashed through her mind. The feeling of a hand around her throat. Lips against hers. And then—

Oh, well, then. Goodness. Her cheeks went warm. She stepped into the room, glancing around, her eyes falling on a desk by the wall. Something in her remembered what they had done in the room, even if she couldn't recall the details. There was something else, though. Something deeper. Something—

"Mraaaaaak."

She jolted at the sound and looked over to a sofa. There sat the largest, fluffiest, crankiest looking cat she had ever seen. No, not just large—*fat*. "Aren't you a tubby angry sweetheart," she whispered to the animal with a quiet chuckle.

She reached out to touch the animal and watched as its ears folded back in perfect ratio to her nearness. "Never mind, then. It's fine." She smiled and went back to studying the room. She tried to do what Yuriel had instructed her to do, even if he admitted it was a pile of crap.

Trust her instincts. She shut her eyes and took a deep breath. She tried to focus on, well, feeling.

"Mrrooowl."

"Center the self, forget all things. Simply be." The voice of an old man whose accent was thick played out beside her. She wondered where she had been where someone had taught her how to meditate. Or tried. She suspected she was terrible at meditation.

Case in point.

Center the self. Forget all things. Simply be.

"Mroooooooowl!"

She turned to glare at the cat. "Shush, you're—" She froze.

There was someone else in the room. He was simply standing there in the doorway, staring at her. It was Professor Saltonstall. He was in black trousers, a white shirt that was barely buttoned, and his suspenders dangled down by his sides. His black hair hung loose by his jawline in strands that stood in contrast to his pale skin. Something about him half-dressed was even more appealing.

By the Benevolent God, he's gorgeous. She lifted her gun and pointed it at him. "Hello. Good morning."

"Hello, Emma." He...left. He just turned on his heel and walked out of the room, heading down the hallway. "Coffee is ready."

"I—" She paused. What the hells was happening? She blinked and looked down at the cat, who simply hopped down from the sofa to walk after its master. Ten hours prior, that man had been trying to murder her. Now he was casually suggesting she join him for coffee. Lowering her gun, she stood there for a moment in silence before shrugging. "Whatever."

Coffee sounded—and smelled—good. She should have smelled it earlier, but she had been hyper-focused on not making a sound. *I am terrible at this, aren't I?* Walking after him, she kept her pistol tight in her hand as she headed into what was an enormous galley kitchen with a large island in the center.

"How did you get in?" He was standing by the stove and was pouring hot coffee into two mugs. His back was to her, as if he couldn't care less about the fact that she was armed. "Ah. Right. You're a pickpocket and a lockpicker."

"The last one I just figured out recently. The first one is news to me. Thanks for filling in that particular little blank." It was very hard to not sound as bitter as she was, so she let the barbs fly. "Anything else you'd like to tell me about myself?"

"A great deal. If it means you'll listen to sense and go away." He turned to place the mug of coffee by her on the counter. He went to his refrigerator to fetch a carafe of what must be cream and placed it next to the mug. "I believe that is how you take it. Do you remember that part?"

"You *asshole*." She was more than a little tempted to blow his brains out all over his fancy kitchen. "How dare you—how—" She sputtered in fury and then forced herself to take a breath.

He was watching her from behind those thin-rimmed glasses of his with eyes that were as dark as they were unreadable. But there was, just barely, a tinge of regret. "I am sorry, Emma. I truly am."

"For what part? Wiping out my memories, stealing my life away, making me a ghost in a living body, or trying to murder me a few hours ago?"

He pondered it for a moment. "Would it be gauche to say neither, save for the fact that I regret both had to happen?"

"Yes. Yes, it would be." She wiped a hand over her face. "Take me to the mirror you have, whatever it is, wherever it is. Let me have my mind back. Let's start there."

He let out a breath. "If I do, things are about to become very complicated for you."

"Complicated is better than this—this—sham of a life I'm living. I walk through the rooms of my own home, and I don't know who I'm supposed to be—who I was." She cringed. "Everyone tells me all about the amazing life I've led, full of adventure and experiences, and I feel…I feel as though I was crippled by some terrible disease. I can't live like this, professor—"

"Call me Rafe." He frowned. "Drink your coffee. I just want to talk."

"Before killing me?"

"Or before you kill me." He gestured to the gun. "Come." He took his mug of coffee and walked from the room. "We can negotiate."

Pouring some cream into her mug, she debated leaving the carafe on the counter. But with a grumble, she put it back into the refrigerator and took her own coffee to follow him. But *shit* if she was going to let go of her pistol.

He was sitting on the sofa in his library, petting the fat animal who was purring and kneading the upholstery between its paws.

"That is the fattest and most annoyed cat I've ever seen."

"Hector is a special case." He smirked. "I couldn't love her more."

"Hector is a—well, all right." She shook her head as she sat in a chair across from him. She put her purse down on the coffee table. One less thing to get in her way if they got into a fight. "I'm sure there's a story there that I *should* remember."

"Yes." He sat back and sipped his coffee. "Emma, I should…I should have told you this a long time ago. And now I see that there is no saving you from your own stubbornness."

"No, apparently there isn't." She sipped the coffee. It was

good, and it made the whole scenario she had found herself in a little less bizarre.

"You came to the city to find your lost twin. Your twin was taken and used by one of the Dark Societies in what I believe is an attempt to bring about the end of Arnsmouth, if not the entire world. But they need the other half of the equation to complete their goals. They need *you*." He shut his eyes. "I wanted to protect you. I wanted to keep you safe. I did this to you in hopes you would go home and stay there."

"You could have probably saved a lot of problems if you had just told me that. I think. I'm guessing. I don't actually know. Because you *took my fucking memories away, Saltonstall!*"

He didn't flinch at her shouting. "Please call me Rafe."

"Why haven't I put a bullet in your head yet? Tell me why I haven't just shot and killed you already?" She tried to focus on the coffee instead of her need to beat him senseless. Her hand was shaking. She was probably starving now that she thought about it. Not that she needed another excuse to be cranky.

"Because you aren't a killer. Or at least, that isn't your natural inclination." He shook his head and ran a hand over his hair, smoothing it back. It didn't stay. "I should perhaps change my statement to say because you aren't *yet* a killer." He lowered his voice to a mutter. "I may have changed that."

She wasn't sure if that was meant to be a joke until he smiled at her. It was barely there, and only a twinge of his lips before he sipped from his mug, but it existed. She let out a tired laugh and leaned back in her chair. "Why were you trying to protect me? Out of the kindness of your heart?"

"Not precisely." He rested his mug in his lap and turned his attention down to the dark liquid. Hector was still contentedly purring beside him, enjoying his absentminded pettings.

"Then why?"

His jaw ticked. "I find myself deeply wishing that no harm comes to you. I find myself caring about you, Emma Mather. And this is extremely inconvenient for me."

That made her bark out a laugh. She leaned her head back against the wood trim of the sofa and put a hand over her eyes. "Man alive. It's inconvenient. I'm so very sorry for you."

He chuckled quietly, and when she lifted her head to look back to him, he was smiling at her, a little bit more solidly than before. There was tenderness in his expression. "I am sorry for threatening your life earlier. I…have decided I can't kill you. As hard as I would like to try to think that I could."

"I guess that's a mild relief." She narrowed her eyes. "Although whatever it is that lives in your shadows might be of another mind—or minds—on the subject."

"They do not seem to wish to kill you either." If she wasn't mistaken, his neck was turning red. Was he blushing? Whatever for? "They seem to have other plans for you."

She furrowed her brow. Then it clicked. "Wait. *What? Really?*"

"It seems so. I believe you feed on adrenaline, and they feed on terror." He smirked. "It is quite the match."

Now she was the one who was blushing, judging by the heat in her cheeks. "I. Well." She put her hand over her face. "I suppose I'm flattered. And vaguely disturbed. How did I feel about this before I lost my memories?"

"I—well—" He was definitely blushing now.

"No! No." She waved her hand. "On second thought, don't finish that. These are the things I don't know about myself that I feel are fairly important."

"Thank you for not making me explain it." He chuckled, but his expression fell. "Go home, Emma. Go back to your father. Learn to live your life again and replace the one that was taken from you. You have an opportunity to take what matters about yourself and leave."

"And my memories don't matter?"

"No. They don't. Not when your life, or worse, is at stake."

"What is worse than my life?" She paused and leaned forward, her elbows on her knees. "What did they do to my brother?"

All amusement or tenderness was gone from him, and she was left with nothing but his exacting and intense stare.

"Tell me, professor. Tell me why staying here in Arnsmouth is pointless—why it's too late to even bring him back in a box and I should do as you say and go home."

"Because I care nothing for your dead brother. I care about *you*. That's why you need to leave. Not for Elliot and his damnable—" He sighed and shut his eyes. "Each of the Societies commands a piece of the human condition, using that means to access the power of the Great Beast. Do you understand?"

"Vaguely?"

That was apparently good enough. "He was taken by the Idol, Emma. And the Idol does not deal in flesh, or knowledge, or even life itself." He opened those black eyes to watch her, pinning her to the spot as though he had shoved a spike through her. "They deal in souls."

"What are you saying…?"

"That no matter what you find of Elliot Mather, or what is left of him, his soul is gone."

"Gone."

He nodded once, gravely. "And they want you next."

"But I'm nobody. Just some dumb spoiled rich girl." She placed her empty mug on the coffee table with a quiet clink. "They can't want me."

"They want to hollow you out and turn you into—" He shook his head and looked off to one of his bookshelves. "It doesn't matter. I will not let that happen to you."

"Give me my memories back and we can fight this together."

"No, Emma. That path only leads to death. For some combination of us, but most likely both."

It was her turn to clench her jaw. "Give me my memories back, Rafe. They aren't yours to keep."

"But they are." He turned his attention back to her, only darkness in his expression. "In my world, what is stolen is the right of the thief. You are either a wolf or a sheep, and shame upon those who are weak enough to be eaten. What I took from you was offered up to the Great Beast as a sacrifice."

"That was not your—" She was going to scream at him for having no right to do what he did. But that was precisely the point he was making. That he had every right because he was strong enough to do it.

Survival of the fittest. It was the law of the wilderness. Those who were stronger, took, and those who were weaker, gave, until they had nothing left.

But by the Benevolent God, she was not going to be a victim. She was not going to let them hollow her out until she was an empty shell.

And that started with Rafe.

She lifted her gun and pointed it at him. "Give me my memories."

"For your sake?" He didn't take his eyes away from hers. "No. And I never will. If you want them so desperately, you will have to take them back."

Tears stung her eyes. "I'm sorry."

"It's all right, Emma." He smiled, mournful as it was. "I forgive you. I can only hope you forgive me."

She pulled the trigger.

CHAPTER EIGHT

Patrick tried to convince himself that what he was doing was the right thing—that any steps taken toward a better outcome were the correct ones. *But that's not true, is it? Sometimes the means don't justify the ends. Sometimes the deeds we do to protect the whole are more rotten than the alternative.*

But in this case, he was fairly certain his head was still above water, even if the whole situation made him feel rather dirty. Lifting a hand, he knocked on the wooden door in front of him. It clicked and swung open, creaking on its worn and rusted hinges.

Whatever he was expecting from the man he had come here to meet, the skinny little Indian kid who greeted him at the door wasn't it. He arched an eyebrow. "Robert?"

"Oooh, you're bigger in person." The young man snorted in laughter and walked into the room. "I see why Gigi likes you. I would wager good money she's figuring how long it'd take her to climb you like a tree."

"An odd insinuation and a waste of time." He walked in after Robert and quickly saw that he wasn't alone. He didn't expect otherwise. There were four other men in the room that he could see, and more were likely lurking elsewhere in the building. Nobody had guns on him, but that didn't mean a damn thing when it came to situations like this.

Every single one of them looked like vagrants or ruffians, their clothes and expressions worn by the rough lives they were forced to lead. His sympathy went to them all, but they weren't the ones he was trying to save at the moment. No, his goals were much broader than the plights of a few cutthroats who had no other options for survival.

He was trying to save the whole damn city, and the souls of everyone who lived within it. Rich, poor, immoral, benign, murderer, or Saint, it didn't matter. By extension, he was trying to save their lives and souls—just not from poverty.

No. He was trying to protect them from being swallowed whole by the darkness that corrupted Arnsmouth. Something that was far easier said than done. "Where is she?"

"Hm?" Robert shrugged. "No clue. Last I saw her, she was in the tunnels along with Tudor Gardner's misplaced Host. But they won't be there for long. Shit, they're probably already out of there by now. That Host would have figured out that she's worth a pretty penny to just about everybody."

Patrick sighed and shut his eyes. He knew about the arrival of the new Host into the city. It wasn't like it was hard to figure out. It was never subtle. But *this* one in particular was interesting. Because *this* one didn't want to play by the normal rules. "He's trying to keep her away from Gardner?"

"And I think he's trying to keep her from getting ripped to pieces." Robert sniffed, leaning on a crate by the wall before folding his arms over his chest in a casual pose. "Maybe something is left of the previous owner after all. Who knows? Who cares? Gigi sent you to me because she figured I'd have information on where Mather was. And we'll get to that. But what I *do* want to know is this—what the fuck is the Church of the *Benevolent God* doing working with Gigi?"

"Sarcasm is not necessary." It was easy enough for Patrick to ignore the man's goading. He had tangled with far more dangerous people than a little street punk with a shiv in his pocket. "Nor do I owe you an answer. Do you know where they are going or not?"

"Eh?" Robert scratched his hair behind his ear. "No. I can guess. And I can guess you're already too late and you'll need to be one more step ahead. And where that step'll take you, I can also guess. But I'm not in the business of doing business with the Church, Paddy. Tell me one good reason I should even accept your money."

All right, that made him want to punch Robert's face in. He narrowed his eyes. "I would tell you to do it because helping me is the right thing to do. That I'm trying to save this city. But I highly doubt you'll listen to reason. This was a waste of my time." He turned to leave, not caring about the fact that there were half a dozen murderous idiots at his back. He had taken on worse in his day. At least they all had faces where they should be and limbs in the proper places. That had been an awful Thursday. "Goodbye."

"Wait."

Patrick turned halfway to look back at Robert and simply arched an eyebrow.

The street thug sighed and rolled his eyes. "You're all so dramatic. Fine. I'll give you this for free, Paddy-O."

Yep, Patrick *really* wanted to punch him in the face. "Great."

"If you want to find the new Host, hmm…" Robert hummed thoughtfully, tapping his chin as if he were coming up with some grand mystery. "Can't make it too easy for you."

By God, Patrick hated riddles. And now he was about to get one, he could tell.

Robert snapped his fingers. "You have one in your pocket. That's where he'll be. But remember to look up, not down."

Yep, Patrick *really* hated riddles and still *really* wanted to punch him in the face. "Thanks." He left without further ado. He tried to suppress his general urge to knock heads together, but in many instances, people made that difficult.

He walked away from the warehouse down by the docks where he had been told to meet Arnsmouth's most infamous information broker. He was, as per usual, deeply disappointed. Emma Mather was somewhere in the city, likely with a dangerous Host as her escort.

If she was stupid, she was trying to break into Saltonstall's home to find the mirror that had likely taken her memories away. It was going to wind up with someone getting killed, likely her. That was probably where Robert guessed she'd be as well. But if that was true, he was right—Patrick was already too late.

Skipping one step ahead wasn't a bad strategy. He had to give that annoying little shit some credit for that. Now he was left with a riddle that he was hopeless to solve. What did he have in his pockets? He picked out the contents one at a time. A handkerchief. His wallet. In his wallet was a collection of bits of paper, money, notes…he had a pencil. He had a pocketknife. He had a pocket watch. He had a small leaflet of prayers that he kept on his person as a matter of—

His watch.

Plucking it out of his pocket, he stared down at the little brass hands, watching the tiny second hand tick along as it went about its business of doling out the time.

Look up, not down.

With a dreary sigh, he looked up at the clock tower that sat above the Customs House by the waterfront.

He hated sarcasm, he hated riddles, he hated being called Paddy, and he also hated stairs.

Today was not a good day.

But before he prepared himself to climb the tower, he would need to go fetch help. Something told him this day had only just started in the ways it could ruin his mood.

Emma couldn't stop crying.

The gun had fallen from her hand the moment she had pulled the trigger. It had landed with a thump on the carpet at her feet. She had joined it there a moment later, kneeling on the ground as she had watched.

Watched as Rafe had died.

He had pressed his hand to his chest where the bullet had entered. Crimson had seeped into his white shirt. He had smiled at her, ever so faintly, as the light in his eyes faded and went out.

His hand slumped to his lap.

He was gone.

And she couldn't stop crying.

It felt like something in her had gone with him, though she didn't know why. But it hurt. Dear god, gods, angels, demons—she didn't care who heard her—it hurt. The instant she had pulled the trigger, she had known she had made an absolutely terrible mistake.

"Kid? Oh, shit." Yuriel walked into the room. "Shit, shit, shit."

She vaguely registered him helping her to her feet. He picked up her pistol, checked to make sure the shell wasn't trapped, and carefully put it back into her purse. "It's all right, kid. It's all right."

She numbly shook her head. It wasn't all right. It very much wasn't all right.

"Ssh. Let's sit you down in another room, get you a drink, and—"

"I need a box." She cut him off. Wiping at her face with her sleeve, she tried her best to clear her tears away. She was failing. "I need a box with a lid."

"What?" He blinked.

"He—he has a cat. I can't let her just stay here, like—with him—she loves him, and I killed him, and—" The thought of the poor animal being alone in the home with her master's corpse made her cry even harder. "I need to take her home. She's my responsibility now. I think she hates me, though, and now she has a reason, and—"

"Whoa, whoa, whoa." Yuriel pulled her into a hug. "Slow down, kid. Slow down."

She buried her head into his coat. The oilskin surface smelled like, well, oil. She didn't care. She was going to fall back to the ground if she didn't lean on him. "I don't think I've ever killed anyone before."

"Probably not. Maybe a deer or two. Or whatever they have in Africa."

"I need a box for his cat…"

He chuckled sadly. "You go get your memories back, and I'll get you a box. We'll catch the cat, and we'll get you on the next train home. Sound like a plan?"

She sniffled. "Yeah."

"Good. I'll get a curtain to put over him. You try to remember how to get to that damnable mirror, huh? That's the next step to getting us all out of here."

Pushing away from him, she nodded weakly. He held on to her shoulders for a moment as if to ensure she wasn't going to fall over before patting her once and walking toward the window. She couldn't help but stare at Rafe's corpse as she heard Yuriel pull down one of the thick curtains.

"I'm sorry," she whispered. "I'm just so sorry."

"I bet he knew this was coming. Or at least figured it was a possibility." Yuriel threw the curtain over Rafe, shrouding her view of his body. It somehow made it much better, now that she couldn't see the empty expression in his handsome face, or the glassy nature to his dark eyes that should have been intensely glaring at her instead. "Should've known before he fucked around with Emma Mather. I don't think much ever gets in your way and stays there for long."

"He knew. Doesn't—doesn't make it better." She took in a shuddering breath and promised herself that she, at the very least, wasn't going to throw up. Maybe later—not right now. Right now, she had a job to do. And her job was to focus, and she could do that. "You, box. Me, mirror."

"Thanks for dumbing it down." Yuriel smirked. "I *clearly* need the help."

That got a weak laugh out of her. She was vaguely offended that it worked. "Thank you, Yuriel. For helping me."

"I made a promise, and it was one I intended to keep. But you're a good kid. I don't mind it." He shrugged as he walked out of the room. "Me, box. You, mirror."

She tried not to stare at the slumped shape of a body underneath the curtain. She tried not to cry. She wasn't doing a terribly good job at either of those things. But shutting her eyes, she took a breath and did her best.

A flash of an image. Of a conversation. And then—her cheeks went warm again. Why could she suddenly remember bits and pieces? Was it because she was closer to the mirror? She began to walk slowly around the room, her hand trailing along the wall, like she was carrying dowsing rods. She waited.

Her hand grazed one particular built-in bookshelf, and

she froze. Furrowing her brow, she wasn't sure what it was that she felt—but it wasn't...

She reached under one of the shelves and felt around. Just by the edge was a button. Pressing it, the bookcase clicked and swung open. And there on the other side was the narrowest set of stairs she had ever seen, leading steeply down into the dark that was so thick it might as well have been a cave.

Letting out a puff of air, she wasn't sure if she was relieved or not. But she had taken a life over this. She had murdered the man in the chair behind her. She needed to get her memories back—to reclaim what'd been stolen.

To learn why his death hurt her so very badly.

It took her a few minutes to find a candle. Then a little while longer to find a match on the desk in the study—a desk which brought back bits of memories that certainly proved that they had indeed made rather violent love.

"Well. All right, then." She cleared her throat, suddenly sad she had murdered Rafe for an additional reason. Now it just felt like a waste. Lighting the candle, she took another breath before she stepped inside the dark stairwell and began the descent.

Emma didn't know what was waiting for her at the bottom, but there was no turning back.

For better or worse.

CHAPTER NINE

It was about a dozen steps down the extremely narrow, frighteningly steep stairway into the darkness that Emma didn't begin to wonder if this wasn't what descending into the hells must be like.

I wonder if I believed in the hells before.

I'm fairly certain I should believe in them now.

The flickering light of the candle she held didn't do much. Without a railing in the tiny space, she had to keep one hand tight on the outside wall of the stairwell, feeling the rough texture and grit of the bricks. It was rather ingenious construction, she had to admit, as she went down the wooden steps that reached far past what must have been the first floor and the basement and kept on going. It was so narrow that most people would have mistaken the extra width as part of the chimney.

And who built a hidden stairwell that started on the second floor only to have it go down a hundred feet?

Rafe, apparently.

And the Dark Society he works with.

She knew everyone had been entirely right about trying

to shoo her away. These weren't the kind of people she should have ever gotten mixed up with. But she had come to find her brother, and she supposed at least she had put up a noble attempt.

Even if she'd failed miserably.

At least she had tried. But in the end, she supposed that counted for absolutely nothing.

She began to wonder if she was going to walk down the stairs forever. And began to wonder if she hadn't, in fact, actually died and was on her way to the hells. *I suppose that wouldn't be the hells, but the veil, trapped in the in-between of neither one nor the other, but still definitely dead.*

Maybe Rafe had been the one to kill *her*, and the rest was just the panicked result of a mind scrabbling for whatever purchase as it could as it slipped into the void of death. She wasn't quite sure if that would be a relief or not.

Her foot touched dirt, and she almost yelped in surprise. Though she found she *was* relieved she wouldn't be climbing down stairs for the rest of time. That would probably get mighty exhausting.

The room that spread out in front of her was larger than she would have expected—a brick circle some twenty or thirty feet in diameter, the walls rising overhead into a dome. From it hung two enormous chains, and from those chains dangled the single largest mirror she had ever seen.

Or could remember seeing.

Which, okay, it wasn't like she could remember much.

Focus, Emma.

The huge wooden mirror frame was as eerie as she could have imagined, looming over her, and topped by the head and shoulders of a robed figure. She was glad her only candle wasn't bright enough to show her what kind of face was shrouded by its hood. She really didn't want to know.

The glass, though it looked more like black obsidian or

something else she couldn't identify, was shattered into jagged pieces. Each shard caught the reflection of the candle and cast it back to her like a billion little amber eyes, staring back at her.

Taking a cautious step forward, she took a second one, and then a third. Freezing, she let out a wavering breath as she watched the glass begin to *heal* before her eyes. Slowly, piece by piece, feathered crack by feathered crack, the lines disappeared. "Well...okay, then. I wonder if that was just as impressive the first time I saw it, or if it's simply fun again because I've been rendered a goldfish."

"They remember things a lot longer than you'd think."

She jolted at the sound of her own voice. That time, it wasn't a memory that was simply playing out in the air around her like a record player. No, she knew it was not part of her strange mind simply because she had watched her own mouth move in the image of her that appeared in the blackened and polished glass.

She stared at herself.

And her reflection smiled back.

"I don't think I like this very much at all..." Her eyes were likely the size of saucers, though she didn't rightly know. The reflection had its hand raised with the same flickering candle, but was simply peacefully smiling, and not staring at the glass in horrified shock.

"Good to see you again." Her reflection's mouth moved.

"Thanks. I'd say, 'you too,' but. You know." She frowned. "That's why I'm here."

The version of her in the glass laughed and dropped the pretense of being her reflection, instead chucking the candle out of sight and leaning her shoulder against the opposite surface of the mirror as if she were her identical twin on the other side of a store window. *"I figured you'd be back."*

"You didn't know? Aren't you the almighty Great Beast of

Arnsmouth?" She hummed. "Sorry. I didn't mean that to sound so sarcastic. I probably shouldn't taunt some ancient and unfathomable evil, should I?"

The figure laughed harder, smiling at her with an astonishing amount of affection. And for all intents and purposes, it seemed authentic. *"I do enjoy you a lot, you know that?"*

"Thanks?"

"And no. I am not the Great Beast." False-Emma shrugged. *"I am your mind. Combined with the reach of Its Will. It can't communicate otherwise, not in the way you would think of it."*

"I don't get it. But I'm not sure that sounds good in the slightest."

"I'm using your mind simply like a...microphone, perhaps."

"And the Great Beast is the voice that comes over the radio?" She arched an eyebrow.

"No. It's the tower. The wires. The radio waves in the air. It is the power that cannot be seen or felt by human bodies. But the microphone gives it shape. Purpose. The sound of human speech." Her reflection looked at her expectantly. *"Understand?"*

"I think so?"

False-Emma chuckled. *"I'm simply your mind being pulled about on puppet strings. Does that make better sense?"*

"Yeah. I suppose." She stared curiously at her reflection, waiting for the visage to summon pointed teeth, or for her eyes to turn to empty voids, or for her to reach through the glass and strangle her. But her reflection simply stood there and smiled at her. The moment stretched on for several beats. "I'd like my memories back, please, if it isn't an inconvenience."

"I know."

"Then why stand there staring at me?"

"I'm just enjoying the company."

"I thought you were—"

"Don't overthink it."

"But you're..."

"I know."

Oh, this was going to get maddening. Which was deeply ironic. "Is my brother dead?"

"Your brother is gone. Don't worry about him anymore. Worry more about yourself and Saltonstall."

"Saltonstall is dead." Maybe the mirror didn't know. Maybe she was the bringer of bad news. She wrinkled her nose. "Do I need to get a box for you, too?"

The figure in the mirror cackled, and once more the smile that her reflection gave her was almost tender. *"You're adorable. No."* Her expression changed as quickly as it had come and sank into something that sent a shiver down Emma's spine. It was vicious, it was hungry, and it was cruel. *"And you are sorely mistaken."*

The dark delight in her own eyes that stared back at her forced her to take a step away from the mirror. "W—what do you mean?"

"You'll see." The laugh that left the mirror in her voice sounded nothing like her. Emma's reflection placed her palms against the glass between them. *"I have to thank you. You've done something I've been trying to do for years."*

"I...I don't understand."

"You will." The reflection tilted her head to the side, the same fiendish smile twisting her own image into something she didn't recognize. *"You came for your memories. You want them back?"*

"Yes." She tried to be strong. She wasn't sure if it would be enough. But it was all she had. "Yes, I do."

"Last chance. Walk up those stairs and go home. Take your life, your body, your soul, your sanity—and let me keep your knowledge. Let me keep that boat keeper's toll and let me shepherd you to the other side."

Emma swallowed thickly. "I'm not sure my sanity has

ever been mine, since—" She shut her eyes for a moment. "Not the point you were trying to make."

The voice chuckled. *"Simply adorable."*

Curling her hands into fists at her sides, she took a breath and slowly let it out. Opening her eyes, she stared back at the figure that watched her, and did her best to face down the evil that was staring right back at her.

She didn't believe in good and evil. She didn't believe in anything but love and hate, kindness and malice. But there was no other word for what stared back at her. A perversion of humanity.

"No. Not perversion. Although, there's plenty of that." Her reflection raked its gaze down Emma's body and back up. *"Plenty of that."*

Now her evil reflection was hitting on her. She made a face. "Knock that off."

"Kiss me."

"What?" She didn't mean to shout that, but she couldn't help it.

The reflection chuckled darkly and spread her fingers wide where her palms rested against the glass. *"Kiss me, and your memories are yours."*

"I…"

The strange image leaned in, and kissed the glass between them, slow and sensual, as if showing her precisely how it was supposed to be done. She smiled again. *"Come on. Don't be scared."*

"I—" She went to deny that she was scared. But what was the point? It knew. It could see straight through her. This strange combination of her mind and the Great Beast. "I'm going to lose something else, aren't I?"

"Nothing I haven't already taken. It's too late for you, Emma Mather. You'll be mine, just as your brother was. And I have such wonderful plans for you. Come here—kiss me—and I will tell you

something." She lifted a finger from the glass to crook it, calling her forward.

All she had to do was kiss the glass. That was all. She could do that. She took a step closer again, even if everything in her body was screaming at her to run for her life. To run as long and far as she could. To forget what she had forgotten and give up all she had ever known.

But it was too late. There was no point in denying it. Whatever was to come, she had already set in motion. There was no changing the course of the river. Tears unexpectedly stung her eyes.

"Shush, pretty girl. It's all right. Everything is going to be fine. I love you, and I will take care of you. And together we shall reshape this world."

That wasn't a consolation. Anything but. "What—what happened to Elliot?"

"Kiss me, and you'll understand."

What choice did she have? She loved her brother. He was the whole reason she was in this mess. And if she could finally understand what had become of him, then…maybe she could have some peace with that before she likely joined him.

Nodding once, she wiped at her face. "I hate quite literally almost everything about all of this."

The monster's chuckle was kinder that time. *"I know. You'll get used to it."*

That time it was her turn to laugh. She snorted incredulously. "I highly doubt that."

"Mm, you're probably right." The reflection leaned in close again. *"Give me a kiss, Emma Mather. Embrace me, and all you wish to know shall be yours."*

She wasn't stupid enough to think this was a gift. She wasn't *that* stupid. She stepped closer to the mirror and placed her palm over that of the creature, holding up the still-flickering candle with the other. The surface of the glass was cold and smooth beneath her palm. Emma leaned in, and her reflection matched her, becoming nothing more than a normal version of herself. The monster had left her image, but she knew better than to think it was gone.

Hesitantly, carefully, she kissed her reflection.

She wasn't sure what she was expecting. Maybe for it to hurt. Maybe for it to feel like a piece of stretchy fabric, snapping into place. Like a door opening in her mind, or a piece of a puzzle clicking into place. Or even just an electric jolt.

But it didn't.

It was as though nothing had ever been wrong. As though the things she had been missing had always been there. She had just been too blind to see them. Like not being able to find her socks when they were on the bed the whole time.

Everything fell into place.

She remembered it all.

Staggering back, she fell to the ground. Her candle dropped to the dirt and rolled, the flame sputtering and extinguishing, pitching her into darkness. Everything was as black as the void. And with the memories came the realization that choked a sob out of her.

Rafe. She had murdered *Rafe*. She remembered it all, remembered his embrace, remembered the ferocity in those ebony eyes.

I care about him.

I care about him, and I killed him.

But that wasn't why she was weeping as she sat on the dirt floor in the nothingness. That wasn't why she doubled over and put her head in her hands, uncaring for whatever hungry Things might creep close and eat her.

She wept because she remembered her brother. Elliot. Her wonderful, silly, foolish, destructive twin. The one whose shadows beneath his eyes never healed, whose voices were not so comforting as hers. The one who looked so very much like her, if just a little taller and skinnier.

How didn't I see it?

How didn't I recognize him?

How was he so close—he was right there—I wept in his arms, and I didn't see it. It was because she had been a stranger in her own body. A shell of the woman she had been. And now all the memories of laughing with him, teasing him, cradling him in her lap as he muffled his tormented screams against her shoulder, were once more returned to her.

Yuriel.

Yuriel was Elliot Mather.

CHAPTER TEN

Patrick pushed open the door inside the Customs House and stared up at the stairway that led to the clock tower. He hated stairs. He was too big for them, and hefting his own weight around was sometimes a literal pain in the arse.

When someone spoke from behind him, he nearly jumped out of his own flesh.

"What took you so long?"

"Sweet sister of—" He clutched his chest as he whirled. There, leaning against the wall as though nothing in the world was out of place and looking exceedingly bored, was Gigi Gage. He should have been tipped off by the smell of cigarette smoke.

"Hello, priest." She took a drag from her long holder, sending the curling wisps trailing up into the air around her.

He didn't bother to correct her. He knew she did it very much on purpose. "What're you doing here?"

"Making sure our little 'partnership' wasn't over before it started." She bent a leg to place her foot against the wall behind her, slipping her knee from the slit in her dress and revealing her thigh-high stockings.

Patrick had to tear his eyes away. He wanted very much to trail his hand up that smooth skin and see how far he could go before she slapped him. But that was the point. She was tempting him. Trying to lure him away from his singular task. "The Host is up there."

"Indeed, he is. Poor thing. I think he likes the ticking. I personally couldn't stand it." Gigi sighed. "Although I think it's a strict improvement. That Mather boy was going to wind up in a ditch one way or another. I hate that he wound up with the Idol, but at least his suffering is over."

"If we don't do something, he might be the reason we *all* suffer." Patrick huffed a quiet laugh. "At least you idiots all hate each other. Makes my job just a little bit easier."

"Clearly, we do it for you." Gigi rolled her eyes. "I'm not here to kill that Host of theirs. I'm here to make sure they don't get a second. They've never managed to summon more than one at a time, and I'm worried they'll finally get their wish if they do pull it off. We all believed it was impossible, but twins..."

"I know." Patrick tightened his hand into a fist and then slowly let it go. "Can I ask you something?"

She shrugged a shoulder in the most perfect distillation of indifference he had ever seen put into a single motion.

By the Benevolent God, he wanted to lift her up the wall, wrap those legs around his waist, and make her care. Make her look at him as if he weren't just an ant beneath her feet. Maybe even make her respect him, just a little. "Why *don't* you all work together?"

"For someone who claims to be out to help humanity, you certainly don't know a damn thing about it, do you?" She took another drag from her cigarette and chuckled as she exhaled. "Power is a mountaintop, priest. And only one person gets to stand at the top."

"And why aren't you clamoring for the peak?"

"Who says I'm not?" She smirked. "Oh, who's kidding? I'm a woman, Caner. Women don't get to stand at the top. And if we do, it's beside a man. Besides, I have no interest in any of it. I have everything I could ever want. Beauty, fame, money, friends, fans…what else could I want?"

"Family. Love. Peace of the soul."

Gigi laughed. Her smile was coy as she watched him from beneath heavy lids that were painted a shade of scarlet that matched her coat. She should be on the silver screen. Somehow, Patrick knew it wouldn't ever do her justice. Gigi Gage was a woman who had to be appreciated in full color. "I wasn't ever destined for any of that, Caner. And I'm smart enough not to chase the birds I could never reach. That's how you run off cliffs and fall to your death."

"I suppose." He hesitated. "But I disagree."

"About the cliffs?"

"That you're beyond hope."

Gigi tilted her head, watching him with renewed interest. "My dear priest, are you trying to *save* me? Goodness, I'm nearly flattered."

"I don't believe anyone is beyond the reach of the Benevolent God. That they are a deity of forgiveness and love. And within their reach, anyone might find shelter. Even someone like you." He blinked. "That sounded more insulting than I meant it."

She chuckled. "No offense taken. You're wrong, but I appreciate the thought. It's charming. Thank you."

He didn't know quite what to say to that. "You're welcome?"

She shrugged again. "So, what is your plan, hm? March up there, slap him in cuffs, and drag him off to wherever you and your white-masked friends put people like us?" She glanced at the door. "I assume you have an army of them waiting outside."

"They have the building surrounded." He shook his head. "They have been given instructions to leave you be."

"Good, then I won't have to slaughter them all. I really wasn't looking forward to getting my hands dirty today." She made an indignant sound. "Who's kidding? I don't bother with the trivialities of violence. I have my own friends waiting in the wings."

"Somehow, I'm not surprised." He smiled faintly. "Why are you doing this, Gigi? Why are you helping me?"

"Because I don't want to see Emma hurt. The girl has a big heart, and she makes me laugh. I want to protect her, believe it or not. I can't stand to watch them rip out her soul, hollow her out like a fall pumpkin, and shove whatever sorry piece of shit crawls out of the aether to take her place. It would be such a tragic waste." She paused. "Besides, I'm hoping that if she fucks the professor a few more times, he might calm down for once."

That made him laugh. He knew it shouldn't, but he couldn't help it. "He does need to relax, I'll give you that. Maybe he'd retire."

She joined him in his laugh. "Now it's my turn to ask you something, priest. You have an army of Investigators who are everywhere in the city. You could clap us all in chains and put us away. Have us hanged for the dark arts you believe we practice—"

"That I know you practice."

"I will neither confirm nor deny those accusations." She puffed from her cigarette. They shared a faint smile before she continued. "Why let us run free? Why not 'clean up' this city like you claim you're here to do? What are you waiting for?"

He frowned. He had been enjoying their conversation. But he knew the moment she ran into a line that he could not let her pass, that was the end of it. And there it was. He shook his head. "Sometimes it's easier to pen the rats than kill them all."

"Liar."

It was his turn to shrug as he headed for the start of the wooden stairs. "We all have our secrets, Gigi Gage. Go back to your club. I'll call you if I need help."

"Oh, you need help, all right. But I think you don't see that, do you?"

"I do." He held the railing as he began the climb up to the clock some twenty stories over his head, if not more. He didn't want to know how many floors he'd have to scale. At least down would be easier than up. "Trust me, I do."

"Come by my club tonight, priest. Watch me sing. I think I'd like your face in the audience."

He hesitated. He didn't dare look at her. He knew if he did, he might turn around and walk out with her instead of following his mission. And if he allowed the temptation to take hold…they would all be doomed. "I'll have to decline."

"Good luck, priest." He heard her heels on the marble floor as she headed for the exit. "And I'll see you tonight."

Patrick shut his eyes as he listened to Gigi leave the Customs House. It wasn't until the door clicked behind her that he resumed his climb up toward the clock. No one was without hope for redemption. No one. Not even her.

But he had a city to save.

A city that, if he didn't act soon, would be swallowed whole. His own life didn't matter. His own soul, perhaps. And certainly not anything else. Gigi Gage was a distraction and one he couldn't afford.

But he wasn't sure he had a choice.

Tap, tap, tap. The doctor flicked his finger against the glass cylinder of the syringe. It was hard to get all the air out of his medicine, but the other option was to risk the patient's life. No, better to be thorough.

Death wasn't insurmountable. But it was inconvenient.

"Sit still," he murmured to his patient. The man in question stilled almost instantly, obeying the sound of his voice as he was trained to do. "Good." The injection went smoothly, though it took him a second to find a vein that had not been fouled.

Treatment always came with a cost. And this man had been a raving lunatic. Now he was calm. Obedient. Tractable. *Useful.* No longer a drain on society and its resources. He would never speak again, but that was neither here nor there. He hadn't been coherent before.

"Orderly, I need you to prepare a room." He straightened, putting the used syringe on the metal tray. It would be sterilized by his staff. "We are going to have an important patient arriving soon. I want to make sure we take very good care of them."

He smiled beneath his surgical mask.

"Very good care, indeed."

EMMA CLIMBED the stairs in total darkness. It had taken her only a few minutes to find the entrance once she had managed to pick herself up off the floor. She had spent a long while sitting there weeping, unable and unwilling to move from where she was. Uncaring if the Great Beast itself came to eat her.

It didn't matter.

Why? Why did Elliot lie to me? Why did he pretend to not know me? Are his memories gone, too? That was the only thing she could believe. Elliot was a good actor, but a terrible liar. His ears went red whenever he told a fib. So he had to not remember—had to. Rafe or someone else had taken his memories, just like hers.

Now she had to go get him and bring him home. She trailed her hands along the brick of the steep stairwell as she made her way methodically up through the inky nothing that surrounded her in the total lack of light.

Maybe this really *was* the hells. Maybe this was where she'd spend the rest of her life—not climbing down with a candle but climbing up with nothing but emptiness around her. She tried to focus on not feeling claustrophobic. In the lack of light, she could see flashes and strange shapes at the edges of her vision. The darkness played tricks on the mind, and if she wasn't careful, she'd sink further into her psychosis.

So it wasn't exactly a surprise when her hand brushed against something that shouldn't have been there. If it had been wriggly or moving, she would have been more startled but somehow less concerned.

It was a doorknob.

A doorknob, smack in the middle of a stairway. Metal, by the feel of it. Decorative. There was a symbol stamped on the face of it, though she couldn't figure out what it was by simply touching it. It was all sharp angles and points.

With a sinking sensation, she suddenly knew what it was. Or at least she had a damn good guess. She would put a whole five dollars down that it was the same symbol Rafe had etched onto his back. The same symbol Elliot had scrawled in blood on a piece of paper. The symbol of the Great Beast.

It didn't seem like the knob was attached to a door. It was just there. On a brick. Being a doorknob.

She sighed, loud in the small space. "Really?"

Now she had two options. Climb the stairwell and get back to Rafe's house and Rafe's dead body—the latter was something she'd cry about for a long time, she knew. Or turn the knob and see what it did.

Turning the knob also seemed like an exceptionally stupid thing to do.

"Look, I appreciate the invitation, if that's what this is." Yeah. She was talking to a doorknob. She was long past the point of caring. "But this could also be an invitation to, well, dying. Terribly. By gruesome means. It's not that I don't trust you, Mr. or Mrs. Doorknob, it's that I don't trust whoever or whatever put you here. Or wherever you go." She paused. "So…with all due respect, dear Doorknob, I will politely decline this invitation. Unless I really am trapped in this stairwell. In which case, I'll be back."

Nothing answered her. Which was for the best, really.

With another breath, she resumed her climb up the stairs. To her absolute joy, she could begin to see the stairs in front of her. Light from Rafe's study was starting to filter down into the darkness. That put a skip in her step, and she redoubled her speed to the exit. When she finally burst from the stairs, she found herself standing right where she expected to be. She put her hands on her knees and doubled over for a moment, struggling to catch her breath.

A new plan was formulating in her mind.

Step One—find "Yuriel" and kick his teeth in just in case he really was Elliot lying to her.

Step Two—get a box for Rafe's cat that Yuriel was supposed to get, but probably didn't.

Step Three—get on a train with Rafe's cat and Elliot and go home.

But there was one thing she had to deal with first. One problem she didn't know how to solve. Straightening, she went to deal with that exact issue. Namely, Rafe. More specifically, Rafe's—

She froze.

Rafe was gone.

The curtain the body had been underneath was crumpled on the floor. The chair was stained in blood. There was no bloody trail leading away from the spot, which made her think "Yuriel" hadn't dragged him away. Or maybe he had, and she was sorely misjudging how much blood there was in a human body.

She furrowed her brow. "Elli—" She caught herself and rolled her eyes. "Yuriel? Yuriel!" No answer. Maybe he was digging a hole in the back yard. Not exactly what she suspected to be the most foolproof method of hiding a body, but what did she know?

Maybe they should fake his suicide. *No, who shoots themselves in the chest?*

She'd call Bishop Caner. Explain that he was some terrible eldritch monster, and that it was an act of self-defense. It was *kind of* true. He'd help her hide the body. "Yuriel!" She called for her twin-not-twin as she stepped out into the hallway. Catching motion out of the corner of her eye, she saw there was a figure standing there, petting Rafe's cat.

Hector was kneading the table beneath her chubby paws and purring loudly enough that she could hear the animal from where she was.

"Of course, the cat likes *you*—" Emma couldn't help but smile. Her brother was always better with animals than she was. Except camels. She was very good with camels for some reason. She turned, ready to hug her twin, even if he didn't remember that was what he was.

Fear ran through her like an electric jolt.

It was not Elliot.

It was not Yuriel.

It was *Rafe.*

His hair was disheveled, black tendrils hanging loose by his paler-than-usual features. He wasn't wearing a coat or a vest. His back was soaked in blood, slowly turning darker with time. He was dead. Or he should have been. Instead, he was gently petting his cat.

Slowly, so slowly, he turned to her.

It felt as though the floor fell out from underneath her. Not because he was somehow alive. Not even because his eyes were now pure black from lid to lid…but because of the slow, sadistic, and eerie grin that grew over him. A grin that was very, very not like the Rafe she knew.

"Hello, Emma…"

CHAPTER ELEVEN

If the floor had fallen out from under her before, now she was in freefall. Emma took a staggering step back. She had to catch herself on the wall to keep from tripping over herself and hitting the floor. "R—Rafe?"

"Hm?" He tilted his head to the side thoughtfully before plucking his glasses from his nose. They were crooked. He adjusted them, carefully twisting the frame back into shape before searching for a clean portion of his shirt to wipe the glass. He placed them back on his face. "We're sorry. What was the question? Ah! Yes. Rafe." He clearly pondered the thought for a moment. "Yes. We think so. He's still here."

"We?" That didn't make her feel any better at all.

"Emma, Emma, Emma..." Rafe took a slow step toward her. "Always meddling with things you don't understand."

"I—" She took two steps away, glancing behind her to ensure she wasn't about to fall down the stairs. She didn't have much more hallway to go before that would be a concern. "I shot you."

"We noticed." He barked out a laugh.

"I killed you."

"We also noticed." He grinned wider, that devilish expression looking so far out of place on him. He took another step toward her.

"Why do you keep—Rafe, are you all right?"

"That's a fuck of a question, coming from you." He laughed again, his shoulders shaking with it. He took in a deep breath and let it out in a rush. "EmmaEmmaEmma*Emma*...what are we going to do with you?" He took another slow, calculated step forward. "Come here, pretty girl."

"I—I'd rather not. What on account of having shot you, and you having *died,* and now you aren't dead, and I am assuming you're mad at me."

"Mad?" He snickered. "No. No, we're not mad. We took your memories. It's only fair you got some manner of revenge. I'd say we're equal, don't you think?" He held out his arms as if to offer her a hug. "Come here, pretty girl. Let's call a truce."

"Why do you keep calling yourself 'we'? Not that I don't appreciate the forgiveness." She swallowed the lump in her throat.

Taking his glasses off for a moment, he wiped a hand over his face. When he looked back at her, his eyes had returned to normal. His expression faded into a slight smile. "Please don't be afraid of me. That's the last thing I want."

Now he was back to singular. The switch didn't make her feel any less nervous. "Rafe…"

"You know what? I need a *fucking* drink." He took an abrupt right turn and headed back into his study. "And a new *fucking* chair." The cackle of laughter that left him wasn't anything like she would have ever expected from him. "Ugh. Add a shirt to the list."

It was with no lack of knowledge that she was doing something incredibly stupid that she stepped into the room behind him, staying close to the door. She would need to run for her life at any moment, she was sure of it. But she was curious. Very, very curious. He was standing at a cabinet, unbuttoning his shirt. He threw the bloody mess away, along with his ruined undershirt.

On his back, through the blood, she could see a black spot where she had shot him. It looked like a hole in the dirt, infested with black, wriggling worms. They were squirming around each other, working to patch the injury she'd paid him. The hole had hit one of the lines of the symbol that had been placed beneath his skin.

By the Benevolent God, what is he? Or...what have I turned him into? She remembered the words of the mirror. That she had managed to do something that it hadn't been able to do for years. She had broken some kind of control he had over the power he wielded. She was responsible for this.

And she wasn't sure what broke her heart more—the fact that she'd killed him, or now the fact that she had shattered some part of him. "I'm going to ask a very stupid question."

"I'm a professor. You'd be surprised how used to those I am. Part of the profession." He knelt and opened a cabinet, then began to fish around inside of it. From some crevice in the back, he pulled out a decanter and two glasses. They were all fairly dusty, but she doubted either of them cared.

"Are you all right?"

"You're correct, that is a stupid question." He stood and, uncorking the bottle, poured them both a glass of what looked like whiskey. "In short? No."

"What did I do to you?"

"We just discussed this." He arched an eyebrow at her. "You murdered me."

"Okay, fine—besides that!"

With a quiet chuckle, he shook his head. "I suppose there's no point in keeping my dignity any longer with you, is there?" When he went to approach her, she retreated quickly. He sighed, placed her glass on an end table, and then backed away to allow her to step forward again. "In taking my life, you upset a delicate balance. And now *I* am fighting for control against the *we* that dwells inside me."

"The Things."

"Indeed."

She took a few hesitant steps forward, snatched up the glass, and then shrank back to the doorjamb. "I'm sorry."

"I believe you are." Sipping his whiskey, he shut the open bookcase that descended into the chamber where the mirror was held with a *click*. He leaned against the wall next to it. "I know you had no choice." He winced as if hearing something loud next to his head before shutting his eyes. "Be *quiet.*" When he turned his attention back to her, he grimaced. "Don't look at me like that."

"Like what?"

"With pity."

"It isn't pity. It's sympathy. I don't know what it's like to be possessed by a wriggling horde. I know what it's like to hear voices."

After a long moment, his expression smoothed. "I suppose you do." His shoulders slumped, and he stared down into his drink. "I have heard them for years. Whispers in words I cannot understand. Words that the more I use, the more power I gain—but the more of myself I lose. Until they were always there, itching at the edges of my mind, demanding to be fed. But I had my ward." He jabbed a finger at his back. "Now I don't. Now I do more than hear them. I *am* them." He sneered sarcastically and downed the rest of his drink before pouring himself another. "I suppose that is *we*, now, isn't it?"

"I met a man once who believed he was four people in one body. I don't recommend calling yourself 'we' in public.

It tends to get you committed. And I don't want to see what they'd do to you." She sipped her own drink. Her hands were shaking. She was beyond the point of exhausted, and she was starving. If she wasn't careful, it'd go straight to her head.

"That is good advice."

"You knew about Yuriel."

That time he flinched as if she'd slapped him. "Yes."

"You knew my brother was—"

"Your brother is *gone*, Emma!" His sudden shout made her shrink away from him reflexively. "He is gone! The thing you met was nothing more than the soul of a monster wearing your brother like an evening tuxedo. Your brother gave up his being to the Great Beast and invited Yuriel in. Your brother's heart still beats, but your brother is *dead*."

"No! No, I can't believe you—he's—" She shook her head. "I have to find him. He just doesn't remember, like me—he—"

Rafe's cocktail glass shattered against the wall by her head. She yelped and staggered into the hallway. Before she could react, he was in front of her, her wrists caught in his hands. "You will burn this entire city to the ground—you would end us all in the name of this childish pursuit!"

"Let me g—"

He slammed her up against the wall, her wrists pinned over her head with one of his hands. The other caught her chin, holding her still. Those dark eyes of his were as black as pitch, but for now still resembled a human's. His voice was low as he spoke, and it kept her trapped far more than his grasp. "Listen to me, Emma…the Idol dedicates itself to the creation of Hosts. They hollow out the flesh of a willing sacrifice and invite another to take their place. Your brother's soul no longer occupies that body."

"Willing?" She cringed. "No…he…"

"Yes. The Idol cannot make Hosts against their desire. Your brother wanted this."

"But—why?"

"That, I cannot say." Sliding his hand to her cheek, his gaze flicked to her lips. His thumb pressed against the hollow of her chin. "I missed you." He smirked. "Murder notwithstanding." Lowering his head just a little closer to her, he paused. "How did it feel, killing me?"

"I—I wept. It felt terrible. I—" She couldn't say the words. She couldn't tell him she cared about him. "I was worried about your cat. I wanted to get a box to catch her and bring her home, since—"

Silencing her words mid-string, he kissed her. God above and God below, it felt so damn good. She had to struggle not to let her eyes slip shut and sink into the embrace. When he broke away, she was trembling worse than she was before.

He smiled, ever so slightly. "That is…the sweetest thing anyone has been willing to do for me. Which is sad, I know."

"I need to find Yuriel, Rafe. Please, let me go. I need to talk to him."

"He isn't your brother."

"I—I can't believe that. There has to b—"

"He isn't your brother!" His hand slid back to her throat. "By the damned, why can't I ever get through to you? Listen to me, Emma. Give up. He is gone!"

Tears stung her eyes. "I will never give up on someone I love."

And with that?

She promptly kneed him in the groin.

"STOP FUSSING SO VERY MUCH." Tudor Gardner placed the lit incense down upon the altar. He smiled up at the twisted, deformed face of the statue that loomed above it. "She will be here soon. I can sense it."

Shutting his eyes, he reached out his hands before him, feeling the web of souls that connected Arnsmouth stretch out beneath his fingertips. "She has begun something terrible—something *wonderful*." Smiling gleefully, he could not help but laugh.

The professor had died. And now something else had taken his place—or perhaps not taken his place…but *joined* him. Tudor had no clue how the young girl had done it. Bullet, perhaps? Blunt weapon? It did not matter.

Because of her, the world would now end.

One way or another.

And it would be *glorious*.

Rafe doubled over with a moan and grabbed himself the moment her knee removed itself from between his legs. His grasp on her loosened, and like the slippery fish she was, she darted away from him before he could grab her.

"Emma—"

"No. I'm sorry. I—I need to find him!" She was already halfway down the stairs, likely making a beeline for the front door.

With a grimace, he felt the whispers once more grow louder. They were a hundred thousand voices, clamoring over each other, each one blending into the rest in a cacophony. But each one was saying the same thing, like each drop of water turning into the crash of a wave. *"Ours. Take her. Have her. Do not let her go. Ours. Take her!"*

Yes. She was theirs. She belonged to them. All of them. The corner of his eye twitched. "We'll keep her safe."

"Safe. Yes. Ours. Have her. Take her! Ours!"

The hunger in him was a deafening cry. But it had taken on a very different need than before. Emma would not die that night. She would not be devoured, her body gone without a trace. No, he was fairly certain his darkness wished to consume her in another way entirely.

For years, he had tried to resist it. He had tried to control it, fighting forever to keep his head above the tide. But now that he was beneath the waves, he found that he could swim. In that way, he was grateful.

"Ours," he whispered. "Yes." He stretched a hand out in front of him. He commanded the power to answer, and like the ocean in his metaphor, it rose. "Have her. Take her. *Ours.*"

Emma screamed from downstairs.

And Rafe felt only joy.

THE DOOR to the outside was right there—right there! She was so close, her fingers were almost on the handle, and she—

Something wrapped around Emma's ankle. She hit the ground hard, smacking into the tile floor. She groaned, stars flashing in her vision as the impact knocked the sense out of her for a few very important seconds. When she came back to herself, she realized she was being dragged. Dragged back deeper into the house.

With a whine of fear, she rolled onto her back and looked up in horror at what she saw. Surrounding her, over every surface, were the crawling shadowy tendrils that infested Rafe's shadows. Except now they were the ones blotting out the sun, though still wispy and surreal. And one of them had her by the ankle, slowly dragging her toward the mass of them.

There was no stopping them. There was no defeating

them. They covered the walls, the ceiling, they squirmed closer and closer to her even as they pulled her in. She kicked and scrambled, but it did no good.

She did the one thing he told her never to do.

She did the one thing she knew would probably mean her death.

But she couldn't help it.

Emma screamed.

CHAPTER TWELVE

Emma was lost in darkness.

She was conscious. She was awake. She could feel herself. But to be fair, it might be a trick. An illusion. Because for the life of her…she couldn't remember how she wound up standing on her feet. One moment, she was being dragged away by Rafe's terrifying shadowy tendrils, and the next, she was here.

Standing.

In nothingness.

The world around her was as dark as it had been down in the room with the mirror. Maybe that was where she was. Maybe everything else—Rafe's return from the dead, his void-like eyes—had been just a vision given to her from the mirror.

But the air didn't have that vaguely musty smell of dirt and brick and darkness. The ground beneath her feet didn't feel gritty like a packed floor. "H—hello?"

Something touched her shoulder.

Whirling, she covered her mouth with both hands to keep herself from screaming. Maybe she'd been eaten by Rafe's tendrils, and this was where they took their prey. What left her instead was a terrified whine.

"Sshh, now." Arms circled her, pulling her back against a solid chest. She could smell the crisp cologne she had come to recognize, mixed with the scent of still-drying blood.

"R—Rafe?" She was shaking like a leaf. Gripping the arms that wrapped around her, she felt his bare skin beneath her palms. He was still shirtless.

"Mm." He kissed her temple. "It's all right. No one is going to hurt you."

"Wh—what's happening?" He had attacked her—well, kind of. To be fair, she had kneed him in the groin first. "Rafe —I'm so scared."

"Isn't it wonderful?" He chuckled, the tone in his voice darker and edged with something that she had never heard from him before. Almost a kind of mania. "Don't hide how much you like it. Like every nerve is electric. Like every touch could be the last." Slowly, he slid one hand up her arm while the other drifted lower, over her stomach and down to her thigh.

When something wrapped around her ankle, feeling for all the world like a snake though she knew better, she let out another high-pitched whine. The sound only drew another low chuckle from him before he shushed her again, his lips hovering close to her ear. "No, no, none of that. You're safe."

"But what about—what about the things in your—in your shadows?" The tendril around her ankle was slowly working its way higher, slipping around her calf. "Won't they hurt me?"

"Of course not." She could feel him grin against her cheek before he whispered, *"Who do you think is talking?"*

Emma screamed. Well, she tried. His hand clasped over her mouth, muffling her. When she struggled, he wrapped his other arm around her waist and held her tight to him.

Her heart was racing so fast she felt lightheaded. Was she going to faint? Seemed like a decent excuse, if a terrible moment.

Rafe—if it was still him—moaned behind her, a sound of nearly profane pleasure as she jerked, punching at his arms, trying to pull his hand away from her face. "Oh, Emma. Sweet, wonderful, *feisty* little Emma. So brave and so afraid, all at once. We've wanted you since the moment we saw you."

She managed to yank his hand away from her face. "What have you done to Rafe?"

"I'm here. We're all here." Lips pressed against her cheek close to her ear, and he settled for resting his hand against her opposite shoulder, caressing her even as he held her still. "I thought they'd consume me when they finally broke free. But they didn't. They never wanted to hurt me. They only wanted to be a part of me and make me a part of them."

She gave up trying to struggle out of his arms. He was stronger and bigger than she was. And the tendril that had been around her calf was now north of her knee, and if she wasn't mistaken, it had been joined by friends. She'd make it exactly one step before she fell back to the ground if she tried to run.

She was trapped. Doomed. At their mercy. There was *nothing* she could do. Her purse was somewhere, she had no gun, no weapon, no nothing. Tears stung her eyes. "What're you going to do to me?" Her words left her as little more than a terrified whisper. And that was fine. That was exactly how she felt.

"We have a bit of a list, if you don't mind." The arm that was banded around her waist loosened so he could spread his fingers wide and press his palm to her lower abdomen before sliding back down her thigh. "I think we'll go through them one by one."

"I don't—I don't want to die."

"That's not on the list." He chuckled. "You really don't understand, do you? That's all right. I understand how jarring this must be. But we won't hurt you, pretty girl. You belong to *us* now."

He turned her to him, and before she could say another word, or protest and say that no, she did not belong to him, he tilted her face up to his and kissed her. It was searing, it was possessive, and by the Benevolent God, it was astonishing.

She would have clung to his shirt if he was wearing one. Her knees would have given out if he weren't crushing her to his chest. He kissed her as though he were going to devour her soul—and perhaps he was. And perhaps that was just fine. If this was how she went...she wasn't sure she had grounds to complain.

Rafe broke away, leaving her breathless and shivering. Cradling her cheek in his palm, he stroked her skin slowly with the pad of his thumb. She wished she could see him—but if his eyes were those terrible black voids from before, maybe it was for the best that she couldn't.

"So beautiful," he murmured. "So wonderful."

"I'm scared," she whispered.

"Good." His lips hovered by hers, his breath pooling against her skin. "We wouldn't have it any other way."

But it wasn't just fear that was raging through her body. Damn her inappropriate reaction to dangerous situations! But it wasn't only the terror that was to blame. His other hand grasped her ass and squeezed, hard enough that it made her jolt and squeak in surprise. The sting ran through her, and in its wake left a wildfire. Her sound of shock turned into something far more shameful.

"Good, that's it." He kneaded the flesh beneath his palm before gathering up her dress so his hand could meet her bare skin.

She let her head fall to his chest, her cheek resting against him. Though the world around her was invisible, lost in the dark void that had blotted out all the light, she shut her eyes all the same. His other hand joined the first, cupping the other half, drawing a low moan from her.

And still, the tendril wound its way higher, and higher. "R—Rafe—"

Nuzzling his head close to her ear, he whispered, "Say the word, and it stops. Say the word, and we'll relent. You're in control, beautiful girl. You are ours, make no mistake, and we *will* have you. But you'll set the pace of the dance."

Letting out a shuddering breath, she felt as though she were standing on that brick ledge of Elliot's apartment building. One wrong move, and she was going to fall to her death.

But what a thrill.

She could stop it if she wanted. She could tell them no, and the light would filter into the room again, and she would be safe.

Safe.

With a deep, sinking sensation, she realized...she really didn't want to be *safe.*

She never had.

Emma Mather knew she was damned. From that point on, there was no denying it. She had looked into the gates of the hells and gone "sure, why not." Because there she stood, trembling in the clutches of a monster, and all she could manage to do...was nod.

Rafe—or Rafe and all the creatures that now lived inside him—let out a hungry, nearly feral growl. His hands slid to her hips; her dress was still bunched up around her waist. She wasn't sure what to expect. But what she didn't expect was what happened next.

He kissed her cheek, then her throat, feathering slow, sensual kisses down to her collarbone. Then he knelt at her feet, kissing her body over her dress. He nudged her legs apart with his knees and placed a kiss against her abdomen. "Come here."

Following his lead as he urged her down, she found herself straddling his lap, sitting on his thighs.

Seeking out her lips with his, he kissed her again, slower that time. No less passionately, but not nearly so forceful. He slid her arms around his neck before combing his fingers through her hair. "Hold on to us, beautiful girl."

That was when she felt it.

One of those tendrils touched her, right at the line of her garter belt. It wormed its way underneath the strap of lacy fabric and wriggled its way north and underneath her dress and her corselette along her spine.

Her startled breath caught in her chest as she clung to Rafe as though he were a raft at sea. "Oh—"

"Ssh. It's all right. We won't hurt you."

Another one joined the first, twisting around it like two fighting snakes but then splitting apart as they wrapped around her body, forever going north. Rafe's hands were exploring her all the same, drifting over her, kneading and grasping, caressing and stroking.

It was all too much. She moaned, half in pleasure, half in fear. She sought out his lips. She needed to feel him. She needed to taste him, to know that Rafe was at least part of who was doing this to her. That he might be…different now, but he was still there.

His tongue flicked against her, asking for entry, and she granted it, eager to let him claim her mouth. She could feel him beneath her, his arousal trapped within the confines of his trousers. She shifted, grinding herself against it, suddenly wanting nothing else except the friction.

Growling, he separated from the kiss. "No. Not this time.

This time is about you, and us, and what we can do. There will be more than enough time for that later."

There wasn't even a moment to feel disappointment. One of the tendrils had worked its way around her waist, all the way about like a boa. But the pointed end was now circling her breast beneath her clothing.

Emma wouldn't know how to describe the sound she made as it squeezed. It was half terror, half…very much not. Rafe chuckled, his hands settling against her hips, holding her steady as she writhed. Though she wasn't quite sure why he bothered—she couldn't move. The tendrils were like solid cords of muscles. The more she pushed against them, the tighter they squeezed.

"Ah, ah, careful. We're like wolves. The faster you run, the faster we'll chase. The harder you fight, the harder we want to bite down. It isn't our fault…it's just the way we are." He kissed the tender spot where her neck joined her shoulder. As if to prove his point, he scraped her skin with his teeth before biting down—not hard enough to break the skin, but certainly hard enough to bruise.

That time, the noise that left her was entirely one of pleasure. The pain from the bite, the fear of what was happening —the sinfulness of it. This was profane. This was perverse. This was *wrong*. And Benevolent God or Great Beast, she didn't care. And she really didn't have the ability to even try to feel guilty at the moment.

Especially as her moan seemed to draw more of the shadowy tendrils from the wings. She felt them wrap about her ankles, slide around her wrists, tugging her tighter into Rafe's arms, until her chest was pressed flush to his.

They were everywhere. Like a hundred little fingers, roaming her, exploring and touching, tugging, urging. When Rafe leaned back, sitting on his ankles, she went with him, knowing it would only expose more of her to the things that had overtaken him.

"Are you ready?" His hand stroked her back, up and down, in slow, soothing lines. "This is your last chance to stop us."

Swallowing the lump in her throat, she imagined herself standing on a cliff. She could jump, or she could walk away. But in the weirdest, stupidest, most foolhardy way…she trusted the cliff. She trusted the *fall*. She knew that when she stepped off the edge, she'd be all right on the other side.

Even if she didn't trust the dark things that were wrapping themselves around her…she trusted Rafe. And he was still there. He wasn't alone anymore, but he was still there. "Rafe?"

"Yes, Emma?"

"I—" She shivered. "I'm sorry I shot you."

He chuckled. "I forgive you. I deserved it."

"No, I—I mean—you did, but—I thought I lost you. I thought I…I shot you, and I felt…so alone." Why was she confessing this to him now? Why?

"I don't think you have to worry about being alone anymore." He kissed her cheek at the edge of her lips. "I don't think we'll ever let you go now."

That should scare her. That should absolutely send her running for the hills. But instead, she rested her forehead against his and took a slow, wavering breath, held it for a long moment, before letting out two words in the rush of air. "I'm ready."

She expected them to descend on her like piranha, tearing her to pieces. But they were patient—careful—slow. She felt one slide beneath her underwear, wandering over her body in seeking, curious touches. Her cheeks went hot as it was now painfully clear just how much she had been enjoying their "attack."

Rafe shuddered, his arms tightening around her as he clutched her to his chest. "Oh, Emma..." The breathiness of his voice sent something rolling over her like the crash of a wave. "You are perfect. So absolutely *perfect* for us."

The tendril slipped inside of her. Tapered as it was, it was hardly a violent entry. She could feel it, though, like a wriggling digit, as it slowly drove its way deeper and deeper. The strangled sound of pleasure that left her was swallowed by Rafe's lips as he kissed her with redoubled fervor.

Gods, god, devil, demons, Beast and angels, what am I doing? She whimpered against his lips as the first tendril was quickly joined by a friend. And then another. And a third found her sensitive ball of nerves and decided to learn how it worked. And then a fourth. Each one moving, each one writhing, each one stretching and surging.

She couldn't take it.

Her pleasure crested into ecstasy. It was all too much. Her body tightened around the invaders, and she cried out, breaking away from Rafe's devouring kiss, as she once more screamed.

It just wasn't out of fear that time.

RAFE LAY BACK against the cool stone tiles of his home, holding Emma to his chest as he felt her convulse in release after release as they ravished her. Not how they wanted to—not to the extent that they planned on corrupting her body.

If they couldn't consume her flesh, they would own it instead. If they couldn't devour her, they would defile her. They would make sure that no one, *ever,* touched what was theirs. And they would make sure Emma never desired anyone else but them.

He had been fairly certain that Emma was depraved

enough to give in to her curiosity and desire over what it would be like to be overtaken by them. But it was her other admission that had nearly sent him over the edge, and nearly sent his plans to ease her into this new life of theirs one step at a time straight out the window.

And she *trusted* him. She trusted *them*. It was both extremely flattering and proved that she was an idiot all in the same moment. But it didn't matter. She was lying on his chest, panting, gasping for air, as they brought her to pleasure again and again. Barely more than the girth of a few of his own fingers was all it had taken to send her reeling.

Never too much—never too little. He didn't want to break her.

Yet.

Grinning, he wished so very much that he could sink himself into her depths, to rut her like his body was so desperate for. He wanted to unleash himself on her like an animal, while the rest of him took her in every way a man could take a woman.

Not yet, though. Not yet. Soon. Very soon.

She slapped a palm against his chest, her cries of pleasure turning desperate. "En—enough, please—"

That hadn't been a command to *stop*, now, had it? That had simply been a request. "Denied." Chuckling, he bent his knees, spreading his legs and taking hers with them. "Once more, Emma. Once more is enough."

Her wail of dismay was quickly broken off with another scream of ecstasy as they worked her body to another crescendo. *"Rafe!"*

He shuddered in shared bliss as he lay beneath her. It was such a strange sensation. To be both himself and more, to be in his body but to be all around them at the same time. To feel each tendril as it writhed and squirmed around her. It was heady and intoxicating. And by the Great Beast, he wanted more.

But Emma was spent, her chest heaving as she gasped for air. She was still trembling, her body covered in a thin sheen of sweat. Her head was still tucked against him as she balled up a fist and half-heartedly punched his chest. "Asshole…"

He laughed and held her close, kissing her temple. He withdrew from her and pulled his newfound power back even farther, letting the first few shafts of light stream in from the windows around them, returning her to the world she recognized. "We deserve that." He only got a grunt in response from her. That was fine.

After letting her catch her breath for a few moments, he shifted, lifting her up in his arms and climbing to his feet. She deserved a hot bath and a great deal of sleep. So did he, to be fair—he *had* died today.

There are worse ways to end a day than to sleep in the arms of your lover who killed you, I suppose. Though I can't think of many weirder.

CHAPTER THIRTEEN

Tick.

Patrick *hated* stairs.

There weren't a lot of things he hated in the world. Even the people he fought against, he didn't hate. He pitied them more than anything else. They were led to think their way of living was the only path forward and could simply not see their way out of the darkness. He didn't hate mosquitos or bees; they were simply doing their jobs. He didn't hate the greedy or the cruel, as nobody ever woke up in the morning deciding to be the villain of their own life story—they believed that climbing the ladder was their only choice.

Tick.

But stairs.

Stairs, he despised.

Leaning against one of the steel beams of the inside of the clock tower atop the Customs House, he wheezed. His heart was racing so fast he could barely see straight, and his lungs burned.

He had to place his hands on his knees and double over,

afraid he would faint. He had to stop several times on the way up. He was in good shape. Hells, he was in great shape.

Tick.

Someone chuckled. "Not an agility man, are ya?"

He shot a narrow look at the owner of the voice. At least the Host wasn't shooting at him...yet. At least he had that much of a sense of fair play. Patrick coughed, took a deep breath, and forced himself to stand up straight. At least the room wasn't spinning this time. "No."

The Host—Yuriel—laughed. The light caught his metallic eyes. One gold, one silver. It made his unique condition rather obvious. With a shake of his head, the Host walked away. He headed over to a set of wrought iron stairs that led to a catwalk behind the enormous cast iron mechanism that drove the clock. It was the source of the deafening *tick, tick, tick,* that resonated through the room each time the gear moved a slot.

He hated it. He hated it almost as much as he hated the stairs. No, maybe they were tied. Though he despised the resonant *tick, tick, tick* for very different reasons. Reasons that churned his stomach. Patrick hated the ticks of clocks. He never had one in his office.

The sound haunted his nightmares.

The Host sat on the stairs and fished through his oilskin coat. Plucking out a bag of tobacco and a stack of papers, he began to roll himself a cigarette. "Want one?"

"No, thank you." Patrick could finally breathe without wheezing. "Quit years ago."

"Good for you." The Host licked the side of the paper and sealed it shut before tucking the cigarette between his lips. "I don't know if Elliot smoked. I don't think he did. At least not tobacco. Strikes me as more of an opium man. Or at least that's what the withdrawal told me." He chuckled. "Poor little bastard, wasn't he? Hated his life."

"That's the impression I got." Patrick walked over to a steel I-beam near the Host and leaned against it, watching the thin man. He carried himself like he was twice the size, like he had been a bruiser in the wild west before being crammed inside the almost waifish form of Elliot Mather.

But he wasn't Elliot anymore. Not anymore. He had merely taken over his flesh.

Patrick sighed. "She'll want to talk to you now that she's got her memories back, I expect."

"I expect she'll put a bullet in my brain is what she'll do." The Host smirked. "She shot the professor."

"She *what?*"

"I know!" He cackled. "Shot him right in the chest. Wept like a baby over it. I don't think she knows she loves him yet." He shrugged up a shoulder and lit his cigarette before taking a drag from it. "She'll figure it out."

"He's dead?" That complicated matters greatly. Patrick frowned. Rafe was problematic, but he was a constant. He wasn't nearly as wild or shadowy as the others and seemed rather content to feed his darkness in the least harmful way possible…even if it meant some seedy drug dealers or pimps went missing from time to time.

"Never said he was dead." The Host leaned back, lying on the stairs as he took another drag from his cigarette. "He shook it off like it wasn't nothin'. The bullet hit the ward he has in his back. Whatever he was, he's not the same now."

"Fuck." Patrick ran a hand over his face and growled in frustration. Dead was bad. That was worse. "So, Emma is dead now?"

"Not so sure about that, either." The Host flicked the ash from his cigarette and considered the glowing end for a moment before continuing. "I took off before it got ugly or weird—not sure the professor would take kindly to me being there. Not sure I…wanted to see Emma's face when she realized what I am. Not sure I'd survive either of them." He shook his head. "I guess I'm a coward."

"Can't say I blame you."

"I don't like this. I don't like any of this—being this way is terrible. I feel like I've got an itch under my skin that I just can't scratch. Like I'm...too big for this body. It makes me want to scream." The Host shut his eyes. "The ticking calms me down. Not sure why."

Patrick knew why. He knew why the ungodly ticking that would drive him up the wall was a relief to the "man" sitting in front of him. One man's nightmare was another's warm blanket. But he wasn't going to tell the Host a damn thing. They were, after all, enemies.

That was a thought that clearly crossed Yuriel's mind at around the same time. He eyed Patrick with mild curiosity. "So, have you come to black-bag me? Got your Investigators ready to drag me away to...wherever you take us?"

"No." Not yet, at any rate. The Idol's newest Host was clearly not ready yet. Patrick had to bide his time, and in the meanwhile, stop another tragedy if he could help it. "I came here in hopes I could intercept Emma before she did something stupid."

"Like shooting the professor."

"Like shooting the professor."

For a moment, the two men just stared at each other before they shared a laugh. Yuriel let out a long, ragged sigh. "Women."

"If I had a flask, I'd drink to that." Patrick couldn't help but let his mind wander to Gigi. By the Benevolent God, he had to drag himself away from picturing her, in all her self-righteous defiance, naked beneath him and—

Thankfully, the Host interrupted his thoughts. "I'm trying to keep Emma away from Gardner. I'm trying to keep her away from the Idol. They want her, and they want her something fierce, Bishop."

"And why should I trust you?" Patrick crossed his arms over his chest. "You're one of Tudor's creations. You belong to them."

"I don't belong to fucking *anybody*." Yuriel sat back up, his features creasing in instant anger. "I belong to those assholes least of all. They didn't ask me when they ripped me out of the aether if I wanted to be here. And they tortured this poor boy"—he gestured down at himself—"fed him drugs, warped his mind. It's wrong. And if seeing that and being disgusted by it makes me a demon trying to ascend to the Heavens, so be it." He spat on the ground at his feet. "Then I'm a fucking demon."

Patrick wasn't sure how it was possible that his heart broke any farther than it already had in his life. He had seen countless tragedies—countless souls lost to the darkness, unable to find the light. He had committed some of those atrocities himself. But here was yet another one, another straw atop the pile. It was exhausting.

But this tragedy couldn't be the last he saw. It couldn't be. Patrick still had so much work to do. "Let's get her out of town together. She'll follow you anywhere. Take the next train north, get her home, and do whatever it is you need to do. Just get her out of the reach of the Idol."

"I would. Trust me, I would. I tried. I can't leave the city, Bishop." Yuriel cringed as if remembering some terrible physical pain. "You don't think that was the first thing I did?" He paused. "Trying to eat a bullet was the second."

Patrick furrowed his brow. He knew the Hosts couldn't die. But they couldn't leave the city? He supposed that made sense now that he thought about it. It just had never occurred to him. He hadn't ever heard of one trying before now. "Huh."

"You know something." Yuriel pointed at him. "What aren't you telling me?"

"A great deal." Patrick huffed a laugh. "None of it's for you to know. Not yet."

"I *hate* that. You're just as secretive as the rest of the assholes in this damn city."

"Hating secrets is something you and your pseudo-twin have in common, I suppose." He headed for the stairs. Down would at least be easier than up. "At least now I know I don't have to dispose of you to keep her away from the Idol. I just need to come up with another plan to get her to safety."

"Wait." Yuriel stood. "Why do you care? You don't put this much effort in for every lost soul. You certainly didn't for Elliot."

Patrick hesitated. "You're right. I didn't." He turned back to face the Host. "And maybe I regret that. Maybe I would have done something differently if I'd known he had a twin."

"Why does that matter?"

"I don't know if it does." He smiled faintly. "But the Idol believes it matters a great deal, and that's what matters." He shrugged. "But it's not your concern. If you aren't a threat, then that's one less thing to worry about."

"What're you going to do next?"

"Go see the professor. See if he's killed Emma and…see if I need to kill him." He grinned. "A typical Thursday."

Yuriel chuckled sadly. "I don't envy you, Bishop." He paused. "If she asks where I am, what're you going to tell her?"

"The truth." Patrick tried not to laugh at Yuriel's look of dismay. "She needs closure, Host. If she doesn't get it, she'll never rest. She'll drag your ass back from the grave if she needs to. Give her the chance to say goodbye."

Yuriel nodded, if numbly. He slumped back down to the stairs, defeated. "Yeah, yeah…I'll be here. Listening to the ticking." He paused. "What does it mean that I can hear music in it, Bishop?"

It means it's almost time for you. But not yet. He kept that to himself. "Not sure." He turned his back to the Host and started down the stairs. "We'll chat again soon."

"Lucky me."

It was a shame when he liked the cultists he had to deal with. It was a bigger shame when he had to put them down. But he had one concern he could walk away from—whether or not the Host was a problem—and so he'd take that as a win. But he had more concerns brewing. The professor might have become too much of a risk, and that was his top priority now.

I hate running around the city like an idiot.

One other thing rang in his head, repeating over and over again like a skipping record.

Gigi.

Gigi had invited him to see her show.

And like the Host himself, unsure if he was a demon trying to rise or an angel trying to fall, he found himself stuck in between. He wanted to go. But sin was always tempting, wasn't it? That was the point. At least he had a long walk down the stairs to figure it out. A very, very long walk.

With each step down, it was like the ticking of the enormous clock above him.

Tick.

Would he go?

Or wouldn't he?

Tick.

Would he?

Wouldn't he?

Tick.

CHAPTER FOURTEEN

Rafe woke up feeling as though he had been hit by a streetcar. Or maybe a train. He tried not to groan through the throbbing in his head. He had never been truly falling-down drunk, but now he knew what being hungover must feel like.

He was in his bed, lying on his back, and against him with an arm draped over his bare chest was Emma. She was sound asleep, her dark, curly hair splayed over her features.

Gods and demons, she is beautiful.

He remembered what had happened. He remembered every single detail of it. It wasn't possession—it wasn't like what the Idol did to its Hosts. No, he had simply been standing in a sea of others. Diminished as a percentage, but not *gone*. Simply outnumbered.

Reaching up, he curled one of her dark strands around his fingers, toying with it. The voices in his head were quieter than they had been before—sated and fed, if in an entirely different way than usual. Desperately, he tried to keep those images of her, straddling him, wailing and crying out in ecstasy, out of his mind. They were both exhausted.

Luckily, the pounding in his head kept the rest of him from getting too excited.

Pretty girl. Our pretty girl. Ours to keep.

Those weren't his thoughts. He winced. Correction—the voices were quieter but not gone. He wasn't alone in his mind; the crowd simply wasn't shouting. Fantastic. Part of him wondered if he should begin seeking out a cure, but he knew the damage was done. The infestation was inside him. There was only one end to the road he was standing on.

Rafe wasn't certain what happened to those who were "vanished" by the Church of the Benevolent God. He had no evidence to support his theory that those who were taken by the Investigators were dead. But the pattern remained.

Each time someone grew too powerful...the white-masked Investigators came, and the individual in question was never heard from again. Perhaps they were simply imprisoned. Perhaps he'd live out his life in a cage, being fed table scraps. *I hope they at least give me pen and paper so that I might write.*

We'll be fine. Don't worry. We'll take care of you, and her, and everything.

Instantly, he decided he hated having "himself" and "himself and others" in his head at the same time. No wonder Elliot Mather was driven to desperation from hearing voices. At least these weren't telling him to kill himself.

Just others.

In retrospect, he wasn't sure if that was better or worse.

Emma let out a quiet hum and stretched. With her head still buried against his shoulder, she let out a half-intelligible, "Mornin'."

Lifting his head to kiss the top of hers, he stayed silent. He didn't know what to say. What was he supposed to do? He had never been in this situation before. Suddenly, he realized he had never woken up in bed with a woman. Huh.

That's just sad, friend.

Shut up.

He wasn't sure who was arguing with whom. It didn't matter.

Say good morning, you idiot. Cringing, he did as he was told. "Good morning, though I think it might be afternoon."

"Great." She shifted, turning more on her side, so she could peer up at him sleepily. "Time has no meaning right now."

He smiled. "That is fair." He released the strand of hair he was playing with. "How irritated are you with me? Should I brace myself for another bullet wound?"

"Why?" She furrowed her brow in confusion.

"I thought that would be fairly obvious." He tried not to wince. "Seeing as…well…"

Rubbing her eyes, she chuckled. "I said yes, didn't I? Strangely, they—you?—were quite gentlemanly, all things considered."

"Gentlemanly." He opted not to tell her that he would have done far, far worse to her if he had been at the helm. But the things that infested him seemed to want to be almost *delicate* with her.

No fun breaking what's ours. Then we wouldn't have anything at all, would we?

Rafe shut his eyes, feeling the corner of one twitch in annoyance. He wasn't sure how he was going to cope with this.

"I know that look." Emma sighed. "That's the look of someone hearing things that aren't there. Are you all right?" She shuffled up onto her elbow before placing her palm against his cheek, turning his attention to her. "At least you have a real reason for yours." She smirked sadly. "Elliot and I don't have an excuse."

"Simply because my madness is inspired by an unknowable horror doesn't mean my reason is any better or worse than yours." When he met her gaze, some of the tension in his chest eased. She was watching him with such tenderness that he felt oddly...content. And perhaps a little less alone.

Which was ironic, considering the situation.

"I'm not sure if that's a compliment or not." She ran her hand down his throat to his chest, fingers grazing over where the bullet had entered him. There was nothing to mark where it had punctured him. Not even any redness. He knew the spot on his back would be healed over, the thin lifted scar that he bore would be broken, a healed spot in the shape of a circle where the bullet had broken the sigil.

If she had aimed by even a half inch in any direction, he'd be dead. *Something tells me that she broke the sigil by design.*

What makes you say that? Damn it if his voice in his head didn't sound almost innocent as it answered his own thoughts. He was used to being in control of his mind. And now? Now, he had lost that luxury. "Emma, I..."

"I cried so hard when I shot you. I thought you were gone. I care about you, Rafe." Emma frowned, a look of embarrassment crossing her features. "I know you probably —I mean—considering everything, and—"

Reaching up, he cupped her cheek, and pulled her down to him in a kiss. Threading his hand into her hair, he held the embrace. He kept it tender, lest it start a fire in him that he wasn't ready to unleash.

When he finally broke away, she was smiling slightly, her forehead resting against his.

He supposed it was time for his own confession. "When I sent you away, when I took your memories, I felt..." He wasn't sure how to word it. He was terrible at expressing his emotions on a good day. And this was a very strange day at best. "I never realized how lonely I was, until I had you so briefly beside me. Your laugh haunted my dreams. I missed you."

Just say it, you absolute enormous idiot. Or we'll do it for you.

You will do no such thing.

Do you understand that we are better adjusted than you are? Do you understand how sad that is?

Yes, I do. Now, shut up.

"Hey." She broke into his thoughts. All of them. Running the backs of her knuckles over his cheek, she smiled down at him. "It gets easier with time."

"What does?"

"Arguing with yourself. It doesn't go away. It just gets easier to take in stride. You just learn to ignore it. It becomes reflexive."

"How did you know?" He arched an eyebrow.

"Like I said, I know that look." She chuckled quietly. "Whatever it is you were trying to say, it's all right. I understand. We have a lot to talk about. You. Me. My..." She winced. "Yuriel." She grunted. "I am not awake enough for this shit. How about some coffee? I need a lot of fuckin' coffee." She kissed him again quickly before almost leaping out of bed.

Emma was only in a shift, and her near nakedness didn't seem to faze her in the slightest. She was many things, but shy was not on the list. "Screw it. I'll make a whole breakfast. I don't care if it's"—she checked the clock on his dresser—"four in the afternoon. Breakfast for dinner!" She laughed cheerfully and headed out of the room without another glance at him.

From the hallway, he heard a "mrrraaaaaack."

"Oh, hullo, Hector. Would you like some breakfast for dinner, too?" Emma cheerfully greeted his cat. He heard a hiss follow a second later. "Still no pettings. All right, suit yourself."

He let out a rush of air he hadn't realized he had been holding in his lungs. That woman was a whirlwind. Never mind the fact that she had been beset upon by eldritch monsters that were infesting the man she had shot and murdered. Never mind the fact that her brother had been overtaken by a creature from the aether.

She wanted coffee and breakfast.

And to pet his cat.

He shut his eyes and draped an arm over his face.

We love you, Emma Mather.

We love you, and you belong to us.

Rafe could only come up with one word to summarize. "Shit."

Emma flipped the bacon in the skillet, listening to it sizzle.

She tried to keep a smile on her face. She tried.

But her hand was shaking each time she lifted the spatula. When Rafe came into the room and walked up behind her to place his hands on her hips and a kiss to the back of her head, she almost unraveled.

I'm all right. I'm all right. I'm all right.

"Emmie, come play with me!"

She cringed at the sound of Elliot's voice. She didn't know if it was just a memory or if it was magic. She didn't care. It didn't really matter.

"I know that look," Rafe muttered from behind her.

"What look?"

"The look of someone holding it together at the seams." He stroked her hair, tucking a few loose curls behind her ear. "Sit. Let me finish. Drink your coffee."

She wanted to argue. Wanted to tell him that no, she was totally fine, and she could finish cooking. But she knew it was a bold-faced lie and one he'd already seen straight through. Leaning back against him, she tried to take comfort in the strength of his frame. He kissed the top of her head again before gently nudging her out of the way.

"Fine," she conceded. Walking over to the pot, she poured herself a mug and put in her usual amount of cream. Sitting down at the kitchen island, she leaned heavily on it with her elbows. The smell of the coffee and the warmth of the mug was comforting. But it didn't do much to stop the tears she was fighting back. "I need your help, Rafe."

He glanced over his shoulder at her, his brow furrowed. "With what?"

"I need to find Yuriel." When Rafe went to interrupt her, she lifted a hand. "Let me finish. I know my brother is—is gone—I can maybe accept that now, but I just…I need to talk to Yuriel. I need to really see it. I need to know how it happened, what my brother said in his final moments, anything at all." She cringed as a tear slipped free. She wiped at it in frustration. "I need to say goodbye, even if it's pointless. He's my *twin*."

Rafe's shoulders slumped, the look on his face one of empathetic sadness. He nodded then turned back to the skillet. "I understand. Very well. I'll help you."

"The Idol is still hunting me, I think. I keep hearing Elliot's voice calling to me." Emma shook her head. "It could just be my insanity, but I don't know."

"It likely isn't. They will want to take you and corrupt you, just like they did to Elliot. They will want to rip out your soul and replace it with that of a creature from the aether, like Yuriel." Rafe put the food onto some plates and slid one to her before fetching forks. It was such a benign, normal action in the middle of a conversation about soul-shredding cults and monsters. It almost made her laugh.

Almost.

"I'm scared, Rafe."

He smiled at her. "That is the most sensible thing you've ever said to me."

"It is not." She frowned.

"I believe it is." He sat down next to her, his smile turning teasing. "You are the least sensible, most errantly suicidal creature I've ever met. I am shocked you haven't yet wandered into traffic, as you always seem bent on getting yourself murdered."

"I am *not*." She shoved his arm but found herself smiling all the same. "You really know how to cheer a girl up, you know."

"It's working, isn't it?"

She poked him hard in the arm. "You're an ass."

"I am aware." He smiled and lifted his fork before his expression fell to something more thoughtful. "Emma, you are in a great deal of danger. Not just from the Idol, but from everyone. Including, no, *especially* me. I don't know what I've become. I don't know what we—what I—will do to you, and —" He gripped his fork so hard his hand shook.

Reaching out, she placed her hand atop his other one and watched as the tension slowly left him. "It's okay, Rafe."

His shoulders slumped. "I don't have control anymore."

Weaving her fingers into his, she brought his hand to her lips and kissed his knuckles. "I don't think they want to hurt me."

"Yet. They don't want to hurt you yet. But you can't trust us, Emma. We'll—" He swore loudly and dropped his head, his dark hair falling in tendrils along his pale skin.

Standing from the stool, she hugged him. He turned so he could wrap his arms around her waist and pull her closer, nestling her between his legs. "This is my fault. I did shoot you, after all. I deserve whatever happens."

"Tell me you'll go home after you talk to Yuriel. Tell me

once you have closure, you'll leave Arnsmouth and never come back." He held her tighter even as he said it, though she was sure he didn't mean to.

Tilting his head up, she smiled. "Come with me."

Rafe's dark eyes flicked between hers searchingly. "What?"

"If I have to go, then you're coming with me." She brushed the pad of her thumb over his cheekbone. "Quit your job. Poppa has been *desperate* for me to get a boyfriend. You can travel the world with us! See all the religions—sorry, *theoretical* religions—you've been teaching about."

The look on his face was as though she had handed him a bouquet of wilted flowers. A lovely sentiment, but useless all the same. "I can't leave the city. I...think I mean that quite literally now." He shook his head.

"What do you mean?" She furrowed her brow.

"What drew you back into the city? Why did you come back here?" He rested his hands on her hips as he spoke.

"I—" She had forgotten all about it. In all the chaos that had played out over the past few days, it had all entirely fled her mind. The ink spots she had seen everywhere that had haunted her while her memories were missing. They had vanished shortly after she had come back to Arnsmouth. She had seen them in the club that one night, but now that she had her memories back? Poof. *The closer I get to the darkness.* "Oh."

"You understand." He sighed. "The venom that's poisoned me is centered here. I am a part of it as much as it's a part of me. I can't be removed from the whole thing anymore." He narrowed an eye at her. "Since you shot me."

"Look, we've been through that." She pointed at him halfheartedly. "You deserved that."

"I did. But the fact remains. I'm too far gone."

"And...what about me?" She wrinkled her nose. "Am I

going to see weird ink-blot things everywhere if I leave Arnsmouth?"

"You'll be lucky if that's the worst of it, Emma." He chuckled quietly. "But you could still be free."

Pondering her choices for a moment, she smiled at him. There wasn't much of a choice to be made. "What, and leave you like this?"

He glowered. "This is not a joke, Emma."

"I'm not joking."

His expression smoothed, and he let out a long, ragged sigh. "I don't know how you survive this."

"I know." She kissed his cheek by the corner of his mouth. "And it's all right. I've made my choices. And now I have to live or die by their consequences."

His jaw ticked. "There are people in this world who love you. Consider them and what your decisions will do to them when you are gone."

That broke her heart. "I know. Poppa will be devastated. But he treated me like I was already dead these past six months while I was a shadow of myself. I won't do that to him again."

Rafe narrowed an eye. "I never said anything about taking your memories away a second time."

"Don't you get it?" She draped her arms over his shoulders and smirked. "That's the only way you'll ever get rid of me now, professor."

Something dark and hungry flashed over him. She watched as inky blackness edged along the corners of his eyes. But he shook his head, let out a frustrated growl, and clearly swallowed it down. When he looked back at her, it was once more the beleaguered and disapproving Rafe she was the most familiar with.

Not that she didn't want to get to know the rest of him.

Them.

Whatever.

"Life is complicated." She kissed him slowly before slipping out of his arms and plopping back down on her stool. "Breakfast is getting cold."

"You are impossible."

"Yeah." She stabbed at her egg with her fork. "And you like it."

His defeated sigh sent her giggling.

Life was certainly complicated. But as he reached out and took her hand once more, she had to admit it wasn't *all* bad.

CHAPTER FIFTEEN

Patrick lifted his hand to knock on the door to Professor Raphael Saltonstall's home. The moment he was about to bring his knuckles down onto the door, it swung open.

He wasn't sure who looked more surprised, him or Emma. "Oh. Uh—" they both stammered at the same time.

Emma recovered first. She stepped out onto the stoop and slammed the door behind her, right in the face of a rather shocked-looking Saltonstall. "Bishop! What a nice surprise." She smiled innocently. "Fancy meeting you here. How can I help you? Would you like to go for a walk? I think a walk sounds amazing. It's such a lovely morning."

He narrowed his eyes. "I know what's happened, Emma."

"I—uh—um—" She winced. "Fuck."

Letting out a halfhearted laugh, he shook his head. "Emma Mather. Somehow, I'm both surprised you're alive and yet find myself not surprised at all." He tucked his hands into the pockets of his cassock. "Are you still human? Please be honest with me."

"I—think so?" She leaned her back against the door.

When it clicked, likely as Saltonstall tried to open it, she grabbed the handle and tried to hold it shut. "No, no, everything's fine. Stay inside."

"Emma—" Saltonstall shouted through the door.

"Stay inside!" But her efforts were useless. Saltonstall was far stronger than she was. He yanked the door open, nearly tugging her back into the house with the force of it. Patrick watched as she staggered and caught herself on the doorjamb before turning around to face him and thrusting her arms out to her sides.

Patrick was pretty sure Saltonstall looked just as bemused as he did. But then it occurred to Patrick what the young girl was doing. Bless her foolish, cursed heart, she really *was* trying to protect Saltonstall.

The professor's features smoothed into an expression of compassion and a bit of sadness as he must have come to the same realization.

Emma was babbling. "Everything is fine, Bishop. You can —you can send away your Investigators, we're—"

The professor placed a hand on her shoulder. "Come in, Bishop, if you would like to speak." He sighed. "I feel as though this is likely inevitable."

Patrick tilted his head to the side slightly. "And run the risk of you attacking me?"

"I won't start the fight, if that's what you're implying." Saltonstall turned on his heel and walked back into his home. "I make no promises as to which of us might end it, however."

Emma put a hand over her eyes. "This is going to be ugly, isn't it?"

"I hope not." Patrick smirked. "It's not even dinnertime yet." Reaching out, he placed his hand on her shoulder much in the same way Saltonstall had done and gave her a reassuring squeeze. "I'm here to help you."

"I know. I just don't know if your methods will work. Or if they'll do more harm than good."

"That's a question I ask myself on the daily." He shrugged. "But here I am. Come. Let's sit and talk. I have information you need."

"Finally, people start wanting to tell me what's going on." She grumbled as she turned to follow the professor back into his house. "If everybody had been this forthcoming a few months ago, I wouldn't be in this mess."

"True, you'd likely be dead instead." Patrick shut the door behind him as he walked into the home. He had never been inside Saltonstall's house, though he had sent plenty of Investigators inside to search for clues to the workings of the Mirror.

He could have "bagged" and hauled Raphael away for suspicions of dark magic and cult affiliations a long time ago. He could have done that to any number of the poor, damned souls of Arnsmouth.

But it wasn't time for them yet.

And it always had to be time.

And sometimes it really was easier to control the rats than it was to remove them.

Raphael was sitting on a sofa in the sitting room, looking forever as frustrated and exacting as he did every time Patrick had seen him. Walking into the room, Patrick smirked at the other man. "You look good for having been shot dead."

"How did you—" Raphael looked confused for only a split second before the math became clear. "Yuriel."

"Do you know where he is?" Emma's eyes went wide as she grabbed Patrick's arm. "Where is he?"

"I'll tell you. But we need to talk first." He chuckled. "I know the moment I let it slip, you'll be out that door like a cat on fire."

"Mrrrraaaacck." Speaking of cats. Patrick looked down at the large, round, spotted creature that was staring up at him from the chair he was intending to sit on.

"Why, hello." He reached down and let the cat sniff his hand. The creature let out another strange, half-strangled squack that Patrick assumed was supposed to be friendly, before it rubbed its head on his hand.

"Oh, *screw you.*" Emma was glaring at the cat. "You fat asshole—him? Really?"

Raphael was laughing quietly. He took his glasses off to rub a hand over his face in exasperation before placing them back onto his nose. "Hector prefers men, Emma. She always has. It's only mildly personal."

Emma pouted as she walked over to the sofa where the professor was sitting and sank down onto it. It was clear she was taking it fully personally.

Patrick wouldn't even bother asking why a female cat was named Hector. It'd be the least strange thing he'd seen that day. He sat in a different chair, letting the cat have her space. "I'm going to ask you to be forthcoming with me, professor."

He arched a thin black eyebrow. "And whatever for?"

"To save time. I don't want to talk in a maze about how you *may* or *may not* be a part of the Dark Society known as the Mirror." He leaned back in the upholstered chair. Hector jumped onto his lap a moment later and began to circle as though she intended to nap on him. He was going to have a great deal of cat hair on his black clothes. Oh, well. The look of childish jealousy and ire on Emma's face was worth it. Patrick tried not to feel smug as he petted the purring animal.

"And admit to crimes so you can haul me off to your church and torture me?"

"I've known your involvement for years, Saltonstall."

Patrick scratched the cat's head between her ears. "I could have had you hauled away at any point."

"Then why not?"

"You weren't worth my time. The Mirror isn't known for its plots for murder and power." Patrick shrugged. "You weren't the biggest threat. Now? Now, I'm not so sure." He pondered the man who sat across from him. No, it wasn't time for Rafe yet. He hadn't yet ascended far enough. "I'll have to deal with you eventually, but I don't know as now is the right time for it."

"You're saying we're enemies, just not at the moment?" Emma frowned.

"Not 'we,' Emma." Saltonstall never took his eyes off Patrick. "Just me. You're the reason he's here to talk at all."

Her shoulders slumped. "Why am I the center of attention? Nobody's explained it. Not really."

Patrick sighed. He supposed it was time. "The Idol is trying to bring about the end of the world. They want to throw open the gates to the aether and let whatever judgment that is owed us to come forth. And they believe that in order to do that, they need both a risen and a fallen child of the aether—an angel and a demon—to balance the scales and open that gate."

Emma stared at him flatly. "Excuse me?"

Saltonstall's smile was thin and unpleasant. "The Idol has never been able to create more than one Host—like Yuriel—at a time. They simply cannot focus that much power at once."

Patrick watched as Emma's expression fell. "That's why they want me. To end the world. Because I'm his twin."

"Yes, Emma." Saltonstall never took his exacting stare off Patrick, even as he addressed the young woman. "That is why so many of us are working so very hard to keep you out of their hands. They think your link to your brother, and your unique connection, will finally allow them to summon an angel and a demon both into this world to hail the end of existence as we know it."

"Will it work? If—if they try?" Emma's shoulders curled in as she sank back into the chair, clearly feeling the weight of the information settling on her.

"Do you really want to find out?" Raphael finally turned his gaze to her, and Patrick watched as it immediately softened. "I, for one, would rather not let them try."

Oh. She loves him, Yuriel. You're right. But she's not alone. Patrick couldn't help but smile just a little at what he saw in front of him. No wonder she kept returning to his side no matter the danger. No wonder she was still alive against all odds. Raphael had ceased to be human; that much was clear. But there was one thing that seemed to transcend even the grasp of the darkness.

Love.

The bastard clearly adored Emma.

And it was likely to get them all killed. "What I should be doing right now, Emma, is dragging you off in chains. You're safest in the church, and I can keep you there legally. I have proof of your dealings with dark powers." Patrick lifted a hand as both Raphael and Emma went to yell at him about how it wasn't going to happen. "But I won't. Not yet. Because it isn't necessary at the moment."

"At the moment," Emma repeated. "Which means it might be at some point."

"When it gets to that point, you won't be dragged to the church by the Bishop or his Investigators." Rafe was staring at Patrick again. "You'll be dragged there by *me*. They want to hollow you out, Emma. They want to make you a husk, just like your brother." His jaw twitched. "I will not let that happen to you."

Patrick smiled. Saltonstall was a temporary ally—a

dangerous one, but an ally, nonetheless. Nobody wanted the Idol to succeed, not Gigi and the Blade, and certainly not the corrupted man who still found a place in his heart to love the girl in question. Patrick nodded once to Saltonstall. It was up to them to keep her safe.

"Do I get a say in literally any of this?" Emma threw up her hands in frustration. "I can make my own damn choices."

"Yes, you can. And it's your damn choices that got us here." Raphael smirked teasingly at Emma. "Or have you forgotten that?"

"You're the one who chucked me into that mirror—"

"To save you."

"Save me! That's rich."

"And you shot me in reply."

"I did what I had to do!"

Patrick watched them bicker and could only laugh. *Oh, young love.* "Can I interrupt?"

"Please," Raphael replied. Emma folded her arms across her chest and sulked. She was unflinchingly adorable, Patrick had to admit. He could see why Raphael had found himself smitten with her.

"We need a plan."

"She won't leave the city." Raphael turned his attention back to Patrick. "I've tried to convince her."

After thinking it through, Patrick nodded. She had come to save her brother but now would likely not leave Raphael's side. And Patrick wasn't stupid enough to think he stood a chance at convincing the young girl to leave the man she might not yet even realize she loved. "Then what?"

"We keep her away from the Idol at all costs. Even if that means taking out Gardner and the rest of his clan. Or we have one other last resort." Saltonstall clearly braced himself for what was about to happen. "We murder the Host."

"What? No!"

Patrick flinched at Emma's shouting. So did the cat in his lap.

"I said last resort." Raphael tried to soften the blow. But it was no good. Emma flew up to her feet and was pacing back and forth along one side of the room. "Emma, he isn't your brother anymore."

"I know that, but—I—that still doesn't make it okay. He helped me. He seems like a good man—demon, or angel, or whatever—and he's—" She threaded her hands into her hair and fisted the strands. "He's still…how do we know there's nothing of Elliot left in there?"

"I understand why you're upset." Patrick gently scooted the cat off his lap so he could stand, brushing the strands of white fur off his black pants as best he could. He walked over to Emma and placed his hands on her shoulders, stopping her pacing. "Believe me, I do. But the professor is making sense. You aren't useful to the Idol if Yuriel is gone. But I've spoken to him, and I don't think I want to jump to that conclusion yet, either."

There was another reason Yuriel would exit the game long before Raphael had to resort to murdering him. But Patrick wasn't ready to surrender all his secrets just yet—especially not one like that.

"I thought your goal was to protect Arnsmouth?" She eyed him warily.

"It is. And I am. Because you, and he, and the professor, and everyone else—you're all worth protecting as well. In your own ways." He glanced over at Saltonstall. "Well, the professor I could take or leave, to be honest."

Raphael snorted, taking the jab as the mostly good-natured barb that it was.

Patrick smiled. "I'm not here to attack everyone who could be a problem in the future. I don't punish people before they've made their choices. And Yuriel has yet to be a problem. It isn't his fault he is the way he is. It isn't your fault that you've been sucked into this mess."

"What about Tudor Gardner?" Raphael stood from the sofa. "Seems to me that if we want to rid ourselves of the Idol, we should lop off its head."

"That's complicated." Patrick shook his head. "He's connected. And I've been given the legal right to do as I wish, but it doesn't mean I'm immune to political pressure. And while he's the most dangerous of that lot, he would be quickly replaced. He has supporters."

A sick smile spread across Raphael's sharp features. It was very unlike him. "We kill Gardner and all of the Idol, then."

Patrick furrowed his brow. "We?"

"It's fine." Emma tugged on Patrick's arm, distracting him. "We won't kill him. Not unless you say it's what we need to do."

"You won't be doing anything of the sort," Patrick replied. "My job is to deal with men like Gardner. Not you. Or the professor. Here's my recommendation—lay low. Go say goodbye to Yuriel and get what closure you can. Then, for all that's holy, sit *still* for a bit. Let the professor protect you. Let me deal with this."

Emma went to argue, but after one stern look from Patrick, she sighed. "Fine."

"If we have to take out Gardner, or as a last case scenario, take out Yuriel...then so be it. But I hope it won't come to that." Namely because he knew it wouldn't. He headed for the door. "A word in private, Saltonstall, if you don't mind?"

The young woman protested again rather vehemently, but Raphael walked up to her and whispered something in her ear that quieted her. She nodded faintly with a long exhale and went to go pout in a chair once more. She wiggled her fingers at Hector and made kissy sounds to try to lure the cat over.

The cat merely stuck up her tail and sauntered away.

Chuckling, Patrick stepped out of the house and stood on the front steps. It was hard not to enjoy the late afternoon sun as it dipped behind the buildings and began to cast sharp shadows across the world around him.

Raphael joined him there and shut the door with a click. "Yes?"

"Do you love her?"

The professor said nothing for a long moment before nodding once. "Yes."

"Are you human?"

He paused for the same amount of time. "No."

Shutting his eyes, Patrick rubbed his temple with the heel of his hand. "You sons of bitches are always giving me headaches."

Raphael chuckled. "At least I have no desire to destroy the city or summon the end of the world."

"What *do* you want, professor? What is the darkness telling you to do?" Patrick turned to glower down at the shorter man. Saltonstall wasn't small by any means, but Patrick had the benefit of being twice the size of most people. Cars were annoying. But looming over people was useful.

"Right now?" He tilted his head a little, clearly listening to the voices. "To spend the evening with Emma doing rather unspeakable things to her."

Patrick's face exploded in heat as he likely turned red. "That was more than I needed to know."

"You asked. And I find my ability to keep them—" He shook his head. "Never mind. It doesn't matter. The point of your question was this—what are my motivations? My motivations have, and remain to be, hunger. Hunger for knowledge. For them, it was meat. Those drives are still there. But at the moment, they have been outweighed."

"By her."

He nodded.

"You've corrupted the darkness just as much as it's corrupted you." Patrick let out a thoughtful hum. "Interesting."

"It would be fascinating if it weren't happening to me." Raphael let out a sad laugh. "As it is, I'd rather like to be off this carnival ride."

"No, you wouldn't. Because you fell in love with that imp. I rather think she's chaos incarnate and will be the death of all of us."

"Most likely, yes." Raphael paused. "You aren't what I expected, Bishop."

"Oh?" He arched an eyebrow. "How so?"

"You're a good man, not simply a righteous one." Saltonstall let out a long rush of air. "I will do all I can to keep her safe."

"Thank you. And I believe you. For that reason alone, I'm not dragging you both away." Patrick shook his head. "Even if it's a mistake. But it's hard to meddle with love and keep a clean conscience. What's closer to the Benevolent God than love, after all?"

"I wouldn't know."

Patrick snorted. "I suppose you wouldn't." He walked down the stairs to the sidewalk. "You'll find Yuriel in the clock tower. If you or the darkness find the strength to push him off the damn thing, it wouldn't be such a bad idea."

"She's already killed me once." The professor smirked. "I'd rather not have her do it again."

"Just sayin'." He began to walk down the street. "We'll talk again soon, professor."

"I'm certain we will. Have a lovely night."

He lifted a hand in silent farewell. His thoughts were already elsewhere. Speaking to the Host and then to Emma and the professor had been a wonderful distraction. But in the absence of the task at hand, another name reared its head.

Gigi.

Her invitation.

He was walking toward his church, his hands tucked into his pockets. He had a few hours to decide.

No, the answer was no. He wasn't going to see her perform. What would the good be in that? None at all. The blonde was the epitome of temptation. Sin incarnate. She was the damn leader of the Blade! What business did he have going to see her sing?

Well, it would be good to keep closer tabs on her activities, wouldn't it? They already had a shaky alliance. Same that he shared with Saltonstall. But if he could make it more permanent...

No, no, no.

He wasn't going.

He wasn't.

He absolutely would not go.

GIGI PEEKED through the curtains on the stage of the Flesh & Bone and grinned in triumph. There was no missing him. He was an ox in a black cassock. "He's here."

Smoothing the silk of her long opera gloves, she couldn't help but feel proud of herself.

"It's showtime."

CHAPTER SIXTEEN

Emma took the stairs to the top of the clock tower two at a time. Her heart was pounding in her ears, drowning out the world like a drum except for the reverberant *tick, tick, tick* of the enormous clock above.

She didn't care.

Her brother was at the top of the steps.

Or...what was left of him.

Raphael hadn't even tried to stop her as she had taken off. He likely knew he wouldn't succeed. She didn't care if it was a trap. It didn't matter if the Idol and Tudor Gardner—whoever the fuck he was—was waiting for her at the top instead.

Elliot.

Yuriel.

That was all that mattered.

When she reached the top, she was so out of breath she felt like she was going to throw up. She nearly collapsed, having to lean hard on the banister to keep from hitting the ground.

"Y'all gotta get in better shape."

It was so bizarre to hear his voice. So similar and yet so foreign. It was Elliot, and…it wasn't. It was being driven by a stranger. A car she knew, with a driver she didn't recognize.

It didn't stop her from flipping him off as she struggled to catch her breath. That made Yuriel chuckle as he leaned against a steel I-beam some twenty feet away.

When she could stand up straight, she took one look at him, and the only thing that left her was a broken sob.

It really was him. It was her twin. It wasn't a trick of her memory. It wasn't some illusion, or some bad prank. Her brother wasn't secretly still out there somewhere, and everyone was simply mistaken.

No. That was Elliot. That was his body.

Yuriel's face contorted in pain as he looked down at the ground between his feet. He looked overcome with shame. He ran a hand over his face, and she watched as tears began to shine in his oddly colored metallic eyes.

"Tell me our father's middle name." She was trembling.

He shook his head.

"Tell me our mother's favorite color."

He said nothing.

"Tell me *anything*. Tell me about the time I fell out of the tree when I was six. Tell me why you hate butterflies and think they have some secret agenda. Elliot—" Her voice cracked.

He flinched at that name as if she'd slapped him. But he said nothing.

"Then tell me *why!*" Her shout echoed against the steel and granite around her. Cold, hard, and unflinching surfaces that bounced the sound back a dozen times before it was gone.

"Why what…?"

"Why he—why you—" She couldn't think straight. It was all too much.

"I don't know, Emma...I wish I did. I only spoke to him once, and by then it was too late. I don't know what they did to him or how far gone he was by the time they took him. He was drugged, on the edge of death, and—"

When she made a noise, he stopped. She gestured for him to continue, unable to form words.

He looked like he was about to be sick himself. He swiped at the tears that ran down his cheeks, although hers had already beaten his in the race for freedom.

He took in a wavering breath and let it out slowly. "He begged me to set him free. He said he couldn't take the shadows and the voices anymore. That death was—he didn't want to be trapped in this city like so many souls. He'd seen the ghosts and heard their torment, and...he chose the void."

"You're lying." She gripped the banister so hard her knuckles were probably white. "Tell me you're lying." The other option was too horrifying.

"I don't know where he went. I pray that his soul moved on. I pray to whoever will listen that he's at peace. But he asked me for—for release, even though it might mean oblivion. He wanted to be free." Yuriel shut his eyes. "He asked me for one favor, like I said. And it—it was to protect you, Emma. He loved you so much."

"Stop." She stormed up to him. "Stop this stupid game, Elliot! Whatever you're playing at, whatever they did to you, no more!" Balling up her fists, she punched him in the chest, over and over again. He let it happen, taking her abuse. She couldn't hit worth shit, but it didn't stop her from trying. "Tell me you're lying!"

After a few moments, he caught her wrists in his hands. His voice was hoarse. "I'm so—I'm so sorry, Emma. I'm so very sorry."

"No!"

"Look at me."

She was shaking like a leaf. She refused to look at his face. She stared at his shirt and tried to yank her wrists out of his hands to no avail.

"Look at me, Emma."

She knew she had to. But she would give anything not to.

Finally giving in, she looked up at his face and into his eyes. Those eyes that should have been amber that matched hers. There was so much about them that had always been different. But there had always been a part of her that would look back whenever she saw her brother. A part of her that always felt like she stared into a mirror whenever he was there.

The bones were the same. The skin was the same.

But the eyes...the eyes were wrong. Silver and gold. Inhuman and metallic. But it wasn't just that—it was what was behind them. If she had to explain it, she knew she wouldn't be able to. There was simply something there that was *different.*

It was then that she knew.

No, that wasn't right. She had known. She had known all along. She had known the moment she had set foot in Arnsmouth. But like the idiotic child she was, she hadn't allowed herself to accept it. She couldn't lose her twin. She couldn't.

Elliot was half her soul.

But there it was. The cold and simple truth.

When she began to sob so hard that her knees couldn't hold her up anymore, he sank to the ground with her, holding her close to his chest, letting her weep in his arms.

He didn't smell like her brother. He smelled like leather, like the oilskin coat he wore, and like cigarette smoke. He felt wrong. Still too damn skinny, but it was just the subtle difference in the way he moved. The life behind the metallic eyes.

Her shoulders shook as she let out a broken wail.

Elliot was there right beside her. But he was forever out of her reach.

He was gone.

He was really gone.

Elliot was dead.

Rafe stood at the top of the stairs and watched as Emma wept in the arms of the Host who held her as though she was precious to him. Perhaps she was, in a strange way. The man who had once been Elliot Mather wore an expression that was wracked with guilt.

There was no way of knowing if the creature inside the suit of flesh was an angel seeking to fall from the Benevolent God or a demon searching for a way to rise from the Great Beast. It didn't really matter.

Actions spoke more than words. And the way he stroked Emma's hair and the tears that streaked his own cheeks told Rafe everything he needed to know about the thing named Yuriel. He wasn't a threat. He was a liability at worst, but an ally at best.

His heart broke for Emma. He never cared enough about his family to miss them. It wasn't a great loss when they were gone from his life. He watched her grief and understood it, yet had nothing to compare it to.

Perhaps that made his life emptier for it. That he had never suffered this kind of loss. *We will if we aren't careful. We'll lose her, and that'll be us weeping on the floor because she's gone.*

He tried not to flinch at the voice in his head. It sounded like him, but it wasn't. Or maybe he should just give up fighting the inevitable. *It'd be easier for us if you did.*

Knock it off, please. Now isn't the time.

We should eat the Host. It's the solution to all our problems. The Idol won't want her if he's dead.

No.

Be logical, professor. You know it's the right thing to do. If we let him live, he'll just get in our way. End him, end our problems. Then Emma will be safe.

Until we kill her.

Oh, ye of little faith.

Please shut up.

Fiiiine.

Walking over to the catwalk that led up to the clockwork, he sat down and watched Emma and Yuriel. The twins. He could see the resemblance now, all things considered. Elliot had always looked like he was haunted by death with dark shadows beneath his eyes and gaunt cheeks. Drugs and alcohol had made him thinner than he already was.

Yuriel looked as though he knew the sun existed. There was some color on his cheeks. Fuller of frame, though Rafe supposed that wasn't hard to do. Simply eating *some* food would accomplish that. He was humming a tune to her under his breath.

And it was the melody that made something run down his spine like ice had been poured down his shirt.

Rafe knew that song.

Though he couldn't place it.

But whatever it was made him feel simply…wrong. "What are you singing?"

Yuriel looked up, brow creasing in confusion. "I don't know. It just comes to me when I'm here."

That made no sense. Why would a clock tower make him hear music? It wasn't special in any way that Rafe was aware of. There was no dark presence here. *Is this place special?*

It's big.

I'll take that as a no. He didn't know what to make of the melancholy tune the Host had been humming. *What was that song?*

When the voices didn't answer him, he should have been relieved. But instead, he felt only dread well in his stomach. Whatever it was that they knew, they didn't want to share... and that meant it was dangerous information. But why? It was just a song.

He would have to puzzle through it another time. Emma sat up from where she had been clutching Yuriel, now aware of his presence. She wiped her eyes, colored red from her tears. Yuriel stood, helping her to her feet. It was clear the young woman couldn't look at her former twin, likely worried she might burst into tears again.

But she clutched his hand tightly. "I don't know what to do," she murmured. "I wish Mom was still alive. She'd—she always knew what to do. I wish I'd—I wish I'd done more. I knew he wasn't well, but I—" She broke off in tears again.

Rafe stood from the stairs and headed to her, taking her into his arms. She nearly collapsed against him. Kissing the top of her head, he shushed her gently. "Elliot loved you."

"This is my fault." Her words were almost inaudible.

"Stop that." Taking her by the shoulders, he pushed her a few inches away so he could tilt her head to look at him. She tried to turn away, but he insisted. "Listen to me, Emma Mather. This is *not* your fault. Your brother's pain is not your responsibility."

"He was my twin. I could have stopped him."

"No." He cupped her cheek. "No, you could not have stopped him. We cannot force people to heal. We cannot force them to be better. He knew you loved him, and that's why he went to the aether wishing to keep you safe above all. Life is full of regrets. You will look back on this and think of all the things you *could* and *should* have done. And maybe there might have been a different outcome. Or maybe you would have had more memories to cherish. But it doesn't matter. We're here. There is nothing you can do about the decisions that were made."

"Are you trying to cheer her up?" Yuriel was rolling himself a cigarette, looking rather wrung out himself. "Because if so, you're terrible at it."

"He really is," Emma muttered.

Sighing, Rafe shut his eyes and pinched the bridge of his nose. "I give up." He almost jolted in surprise as Emma hugged him in response, wrapping her arms around his midsection and squeezing.

He stroked her hair and let her gather her wits. When she stepped away from him, she looked just a little bit more like the Emma he knew. Barely. But the pieces were there.

Annoyed, she wiped at her face. "I'm going to be crying for a while."

"That's acceptable." Rafe took his glasses off to clean them with his handkerchief.

"I wasn't asking for permission, professor," Emma grumbled.

Yuriel chuckled. "I don't care what people say. You two are adorable together."

Emma turned to the Host, her eyes flicking back and forth between Yuriel's metallic ones, searching as if in one last attempt to find some shard of Elliot looking back at her. Her shoulders slumped a moment later. "I need a stiff drink."

"I can get behind that." Yuriel placed his cigarette between his lips.

Emma reached out, plucked the cigarette out of his mouth, and tossed it to the ground. "No. That's disgusting, and it's bad for you. You won't be doing that shit around me."

"I—" Yuriel blinked. "Um. Yes, ma'am." He paused. "I don't know what that means, exactly, but—"

"It means we're friends. No, it means you're *family*. You

might not be my brother, but he gave you his life, and he made you promise to protect me. So, you're going to come with us."

Rafe cleared his throat. "Excuse me?"

"You have plenty of rooms." She glared up at him with such ire that Rafe wondered if he had actually offended her. "And your other *friends* will just need to learn to play nice with others."

We'll play real nice with you, we promise. But the Host is still up for debate. Although, the more the merrier, right? Wait...does that still count as incest?

It took every ounce of strength Rafe had in his body not to react to what the voices were saying. Luckily, Emma was already walking away from them, storming toward the stairs with all the anger in the world.

"Seems like the decision's been made," Yuriel mumbled to him.

"Seems so."

"Are we going to have problems, you 'n me, professor?" Yuriel looked down at his crushed cigarette and sighed. "I'm gonna miss the tobacco."

"I'm not entirely sure, to be frank." Rafe pulled a small container from his pocket and flicked it open, offering the other man a toothpick. "I am recently returned from the dead with a bit more company in my head than before, so such matters are a bit unpredictable at the moment."

"Fair." Yuriel took a toothpick from the container and tucked it between his teeth. "Easiest way to fix this problem is removing me from the equation."

"I know."

"You'd be smart to push me off the clock tower." Yuriel eyed him narrowly.

"It's come up in conversation." Rafe tilted his head thoughtfully. "Why not kill yourself, I wonder?"

"I have work to do here. I don't know what it is. But I have work to do. Not least of all..." He jerked his head toward the stairs where Emma had gone. "Keeping her safe like I promised."

"I fear she'll be the doom of us all."

Emma angrily appeared at the top of the stairs again. "Are you two idiots coming or not?" She stormed back down a second time.

Yuriel grunted. "Ain't that the truth."

THE WALK down the stairs was done in silence. Emma was fine with that. She was on the brink of another breakdown. Her hands were shaking, and she suddenly wanted a steak dinner and an entire bottle of vodka.

Her day couldn't get any worse.

And it was at exactly that moment that she learned why she should never challenge the universe like that. Because as she reached out to grab the handle to leave the building, Yuriel snatched her wrist. "Wait."

"What?" She blinked.

Yuriel drew one of his pistols from the holster. "Listen."

"Emmie, come play with me!"

Emma froze, her eyes going wide. Tears welled in her again. "No."

"Emma, join me. Come be with me. We can be free together! I'm so happy now. You can be happy, too."

"Elliot...?" She went for the doorknob again.

"It's a lie." Yuriel yanked her back. "It's all a lie. He's gone, Emma. Your brother is dead. He's *gone*. That isn't him. They're just tricking you—" The Host let out a strangled *hurk* as Rafe grabbed him by the throat and slammed him up against the wall next to the door.

"The Idol is here. This was a trap!" Rafe snarled. "Tell me one good reason why it wasn't you who set it and why I shouldn't peel you like an orange."

"I—" Yuriel gagged. "Made a promise—"

"Stop it." Neither of them heard her. Or they didn't care.

"Promises. *Right.* What about the promise you made to the Idol?"

"Fuck them." Yuriel put his gun against the underside of Rafe's chin. "Don't make me shoot you."

"Oh, please." Rafe grinned, a sick and sadistic expression she recognized as his other half. Or halves, maybe. "Make our day…"

She didn't need to see Rafe's face to know his eyes had gone as black as the void. Yuriel's expression of horror was enough. "What the fuck *are* you?"

"The thing that's going to eat you." Rafe grinned.

"Enough!" She shoved the professor hard enough to send him staggering a step. Not because she was that strong but simply because she'd caught him off guard. "Both of you, *stop it.*" Pointing at the door, she turned to Yuriel, feeling all at once frantic, angry, and terrified. "Is that really my brother?"

"No." Yuriel coughed.

"Eeemmiiiee!"

"How do I know you're telling the truth?" She was shaking again. "How do I know that isn't really him?"

"You'll have to trust me, stupid as that sounds." Yuriel pulled his other gun from his holster and checked the ammunition in both. "Simple fact is, the Idol has us surrounded. And if we don't want you to get turned into whatever the fuck I am, we need to get out of here."

Rafe cracked his neck from one side to the other and looked out the window. The sun had long since set, casting the city in darkness. "Shoot the lamps."

"Huh?" Yuriel shook his head in confusion. "What good is that gonna—"

"Just do as we say. Shoot the lamps. Emma, stay here. Whatever you hear, for once in your damn life, will you stay put?" Rafe's tone was harsh, but he seemed almost manic. No, it was gleeful. Whatever was about to happen, he looked almost giddy about it.

That scared her worse than the disembodied voice of her brother still calling to her from the street. Or the fact that Rafe's eyes had gone as dark as the night sky beyond. Nodding numbly, she walked to the stone wall and leaned against it.

"Shoot the lamps." Yuriel sighed and moved to stand in front of the door. Rafe joined him at his side. The Host glanced at the professor. "This gets bad, you know what you need to do. They can't have both of us."

"Trust us. We won't hesitate." Rafe smirked. "Not even in the slightest."

Yuriel made a face. "I don't think I'm comfortable with this."

"Not sure as we have a choice." Rafe gestured to the door. "After you."

Yuriel threw open the door. She ducked away from the booming echoes of gunfire. But soon it was drowned out by the sound of screams. High-pitched, terrible, inhuman sounds that should have every right to shatter the glass in the windows.

But through it all, she could hear him calling to her.

"Emma, come with me. I miss you. I love you."

She sank to the floor, her hands over her ears, and wept.

"I will always love you, Emma."

CHAPTER SEVENTEEN

"I don't want you giving anybody any trouble."

Patrick stared down at the man at the door. He knew his name. He knew everything there was to know about Gigi Gage's right-hand man, Mykel. Or perhaps left-hand would be more appropriate. Mykel was the enforcer and the *fixer* who got his hands dirty. And Patrick suspected the man was also fiercely protective of his boss.

"I'm not here to bother your patrons." Patrick straightened his shoulders, cracking his back. He hated stooping, but the hallway that went into the nightclub was small, and the ceiling was too close to his head for comfort. "I don't care if they're drinking."

"Lot more goes on here than that, and you know it." Mykel glared up at him. He was likely trying to intimidate him.

Patrick rolled his eyes. "Right. And I don't care about any of *that*, either." Homosexuality, drugs, alcohol—all illegal in the eyes of the State. And the Church, to be fair, had less than favorable views on those topics.

But that wasn't his job.

His job was to keep the city of Arnsmouth from being devoured by the Great Beast. "I'll let you in on a secret, Mykel. I don't give two *fucks* what people gotta do to stay afloat in this world. Let 'em love who they want. Let 'em drink and snort whatever they want if it gets them to the next day. I have bigger problems."

Mykel huffed. "Right. Well. Doesn't matter what I think, anyway." He shook his head. "Boss's orders. She even saved you a table." He pointed into the lounge. There, right by the edge of the stage that protruded into the arrangement of seats like a fashion catwalk, was a single empty table surrounded by a packed crowd. It was the only empty spot he could see.

"Of course, she did." He fought the urge to fidget as he walked away and headed to the table. He wasn't a nervous man, but here he was. With everything he had done in his life, with all the terrible deeds he'd carried out, why was he nervous *now*? What was different?

You're playing with fire, you big idiot. That's why. You're playing with fire, and you want to get burned.

No. That wasn't the case. He was here to learn. To manipulate. If he could control Gigi Gage, if he could get some sort of power over her, then he would control one of the five Dark Societies of Arnsmouth. That was an opportunity that was too important to pass up, even if it was a dangerous one.

A temptation too big to ignore.

He sighed again as he sat down at the table, feeling the chair sag a little under his weight. He was used to it. He'd gone through more than a few pieces of furniture in his day, just by benefit of his size. It meant he always sat down carefully.

It was hard to ignore the looks from the people around him, and how they suddenly shifted to turn their backs to him. It was like they were trying to hide the flasks they kept pulling from their coats.

He really, really didn't care. Hells, he could use a damn drink himself. It was a stupid law, one he hoped would be repealed sooner rather than later. But he had larger fish to fry than to worry about whether or not people were having fun.

Shifting his attention back to the stage, he ignored the continued stares from the people at the tables around him. He was used to it. His mother had jokingly called him an eyesore growing up. Scratching at the stubble on his chin, he smiled at the memory of her. It was hard to hide and easy to stick out when one was nearly seven feet tall and three feet wide at the shoulder. *"Get used to people lookin' at you. You'd have an easier time getting a barn to blend into a field,"* she had always said. And it was true.

By the Benevolent God, he missed his mother. He figured he always would. But she was at peace now, with their maker, and was certainly happy. He would see her again. And if he kept making stupid decisions like this one, sitting at the club owned by a notorious leader of a Dark Society, probably sooner rather than later.

Someone brushed against his arm as they leaned over his table. "On the house, sweetheart." The waitress was dressed to the nines, decked out to the full extent of fashion. Crimson lips turned into a smile as she plonked a drink down in front of him. "Enjoy the show."

"Thank—" he began. She was already gone. "—you." He sighed.

Looking at the drink in front of him, he laughed. *I hate you a little, Gigi Gage. Or maybe this is Mykel's doing. Either way.* The thing sitting in front of him on the white tablecloth was quite simply the girliest drink he had ever seen.

It was an offensive shade of pink that transitioned at the

bottom into an equally obscene shade of turquoise. It had curls of orange skin sticking off it in various directions. Small toothpicks held an array of fruit that were jabbed into the ice at the top.

With a shrug, he plucked one of the toothpicks out of the drink and began munching away on the fruit. Glancing over at a table beside him, he saw one of the couples was now staring at him again. "What? I like fruit."

They nervously went back to what they were doing.

Chuckling, he returned to his drink. It wasn't a lie—he *did* like fruit.

The lights dimmed, and the humor of his situation was lost as electric spotlights loudly clicked on, illuminating the center of the closed curtains. The crowd fell silent. There was no announcement. There wasn't a need. Everyone knew who was about to perform.

"Love, you didn't do right by me…"

He recognized the voice. He had never heard Gigi sing, but there was no doubt in his mind who it belonged to. The curtains parted, and his breath hitched. Hells, his heart might have stopped entirely.

He wasn't sure if it was the sequins on the black dress that drew his attention to her, or the way it clung to every curve on her body. It was an almost scandalous dress, and certainly ahead of the boxy designs of the day.

Gigi Gage took a step forward, her white opera gloves almost matching her platinum hair, both in stark contrast to the dress that trailed behind her like a pool of shimmering darkness.

At some point, Patrick remembered to breathe.

She was the most beautiful thing he had ever seen.

The most dangerous.

And the most beautiful.

Like a venomous snake. Graceful and perfect but designed for a single purpose—to lure in the foolish.

And he was an *enormous* fool.

He barely heard the lyrics to the song. He didn't care. He couldn't look away from her, fixated, as she walked out onto the stage. But true to her nature, the performance was hardly as he would have expected it to go. She stepped from the stage right onto a nearby table. A gentleman shot up from his chair to help her as she used his seat to reach the floor, now walking amongst the audience as she sang.

And then, all at once, her focus was on him.

If he could have melted into the floor. If he could have hidden. If he could have jumped up from his seat and run for his life, he would have.

But he was trapped. Trapped by those eyes that pinned him to the spot. She walked up to him, her crooning voice hypnotizing him. A brush of silk against his face had him jolting in surprise as she trailed her gloved hand down his cheek. And then to his throat.

His heart was pounding in his ears, nearly drowning out everything else around him. Her hand ran down his neck, as if searching out the pulse. The room felt far too hot, far too close.

Patrick didn't know what to do.

She leaned in, as if to kiss him, her song hesitating. He could smell her, like lavender and roses.

But at the last second, she pulled away. And with it, lifted the chain he wore that bore his cross from around his neck. She'd stolen his cross!

"Hey—" There was no use. He wasn't sure why he bothered.

She placed her fingers to his lips, shushing him, as she continued to sing. The crowd around her chuckled as she stepped away, slipping the chain around her own neck to toy with the double-sided cross that dangled at the end.

She sauntered back onto the stage the same way she got down, climbing on a chair then the table to reach the platform. Standing on the stage, her back to the audience, she finished her song just as the curtains closed behind her.

The crowd applauded.

And he simply sat there like the idiot that he was.

GIGI TWIRLED the metal cross around on her fingers as she walked backstage. She was smiling, and knew she likely looked entirely too proud of herself. She'd usually scold her other singers for looking so pleased with their performances, but she couldn't help it. That had gone spectacularly.

And oh, the look on the poor priest's face. To describe him as a deer in the headlights—*more like an ox, with his size*—wouldn't do it justice. It was as though he had never seen a woman before that moment. It was as though she had been the most amazing thing he had ever witnessed.

And by the Great Beast, it had felt so good. She knew he wasn't an innocent man. He wasn't a complete fish in the barrel. She'd heard the rumors of all her "compatriots" who had been mysteriously vanished by Bishop Caner and his league of Investigators.

Bishop Patrick Caner had also, as far as the story went, once rooted out a den that belonged to the Candle and—or so Robert told her—punched a man's head in until there was barely anything left of him.

All in the name of his holy so-called Benevolent God.

And they call us *a cult.*

She huffed as she walked into her dressing room. She was wearing the stolen necklace and intended to keep it around her neck until Caner came back to fetch it. And he would. She *knew* he would. He wouldn't be able to help himself.

Just as she wouldn't be able to help herself, either.

He was such a tasty temptation. Never in a million years would she have guessed he would be so easy to play with, so simple to lure in. She stripped out of the slinky sequin gown, ditched her gloves, and decided that going with something more sinful—something more risqué—would do the job far better.

Stripping naked, she donned a sheer dressing gown made of chiffon. Just enough layers to obscure, but not enough to hide. Perfect. Lying down on the chaise by the wall, she arranged herself *just so*. The girls had already brought in some drinks, and she had told them to leave the bottle. Expensive Irish whiskey. She figured it was an amusing jab at the redhead.

Plucking up a cigarette, she lit it, draping the fur over her body to leave just a little more to the imagination for the moment, and waited.

It was a dangerous game, playing with the priest. He could drag her off and black-bag her like so many of her friends and compatriots over the years. He could murder her outright or put her on trial and have her hanged for her crimes. He knew who she was. He knew what she was. And she, in turn, knew him.

A man with eyes as green as a field of grass on a summer day. A man whose smile twisted a knot in her stomach in a way that she hated and adored. A man who said she was not beyond hope. And that, right there, was why she wanted to tear him down. She wanted to corrupt him, to drag him into sin, to teach him how far beyond saving Arnsmouth really was.

How far beyond saving *she* was.

Because how dare he say that? How dare he believe that? Her! Gigi Gage! He thought he could help her? Please.

She didn't have to wait long.

There was a knock on the door.

"The Bishop is here to see you, Boss," Mykel called through the door.

She smiled. "Let him in."

CHAPTER EIGHTEEN

Emma wasn't sure when she stopped crying. She wasn't sure when she just went numb to the sound of screams. Some human...most not.

She wasn't sure when someone picked her up off the ground, steadying her on her feet, and began shushing her quietly, telling her it would all be all right. The shape of the body was familiar to her—thin like hers, maybe just a tiny bit taller—the smell of oiled leather and tobacco was not.

Elliot. Yuriel.

Her brother was dead. It was going to take some time to get used to that.

Tears would have come again if she could have managed it. She was shaking too hard. She couldn't even remember much of what had just happened. Raphael and Yuriel had stormed out the door. There had been gunfire. Screams. Shrieks of creatures she knew would give her nightmares, if not send her off to Arnsmouth Asylum as a drooling lunatic.

But she did remember the laughter. *His* laughter.

Over the din of the battle, over the shattering glass—the bits of which were now crunching underneath her feet as

Yuriel carefully led her outside—had been the sound of Rafe. Cackling like a madman, like the villain of some badly acted melodrama. But the sound hadn't been entirely him. Something else had been laughing along with him. Like waves crashing against a rock cliff, bass and inhuman.

But filled with the joy of chaos.

And there he was, standing at the top of the stairs leading to the Customs House. His head was lowered, his dark hair a mess of strands that hung down against his pale face. He was breathing heavily, his hands balled into fists at his sides.

Yuriel hugged her close. "It's all right, Emma. It's going to be all right."

Somehow, she very much doubted that. The street was carnage—lamp posts bent and warped, benches overturned, a parked car was flattened. Windows were shattered.

One lamp post looked like it had been grabbed by something's very large hand and squeezed, the indents of giant fingers all that was left of whatever had done it.

And then there was the smell.

The air reeked of blood and ozone, as though lightning had just struck the ground. But she couldn't see anything anywhere—no corpses, no blood, no singes on the pavement. Just the aftermath of a fight left behind on stone and steel.

"Rafe?" Her voice sounded so small and hoarse. Maybe she'd been screaming during the fight. Or maybe that was from all the sobbing she had done at realizing her twin was as good as dead. She honestly didn't know. She supposed it didn't really matter.

Loudly, he cracked his neck, tilting his head to one side and then the other. But he didn't answer.

She suspected she knew why. Either it was too noisy in his head to hear her, or…Rafe wasn't home right now. She gently pushed away from Yuriel, and when he tried to stop her, she nodded at him once. She smiled faintly at the whatever-he-really-was, hoping he understood what she was trying to say.

He sighed but let her go.

It was dangerous. She knew Rafe was a monster. She had seen it herself. And now, with what he'd just done to a hoard of *other* monsters, she had all the proof she would ever need that he was capable of terrible things. Who knew how much of the devastation had been his doing?

Carefully, waiting for him to lash out at her at any moment, she stepped around in front of him.

His eyes were shut, and his head was lowered. His expression was peaceful, which somehow only made things worse. His glasses weren't even crooked. Except for his gradually slowing breathing and mussed hair, he looked like nothing had happened.

Well, all right. His tie was a little off. Reaching up, she carefully straightened it for him.

That got his attention. Inky, full-black eyes opened to watch her idly as she fixed his tie and tucked it back into his vest. Thinly, he smiled. "Thank you, Emma."

The way he said it sent a shiver down her spine. It was clear that *they* were in control, even if the eyes hadn't been a dead giveaway. "Did we win?"

"We won." He sniffed dismissively. "For now." He lifted his head to look over her to the damage that the fight had caused. He tilted his head slowly to one side. "And we made a mess. Oh, well. We cleaned up as much of it as we could. Sadly, we aren't in the business of eating rocks and metal." He shifted his gaze back down to her—or at least she assumed so. It was hard to tell when he had no irises or pupils. "But you already knew that." His smile was devilish. "Didn't you?"

It looked as though he planned to eat her. And she knew he could. She felt so damn small, and she tried her damnedest not to shrink away from him in fear. He was a predator—running only made it worse. "Yeah..."

"Oh, don't look at us like that." He lifted a hand, and she barely kept herself from flinching as he placed his palm to her cheek, stroking his thumb along her skin. "We kept you safe, didn't we?"

That was true. She had to give them that. She nodded and found herself staring at his black-and-burgundy paisley tie. "What now?"

"Unsure." Carefully, as if he was worried that he was going to startle her, he wrapped an arm around her waist and pulled her closer to him. "The Idol couldn't very well pass up the opportunity to come collect their wayward Host and his hopeful second half. We doubt they'll stop simply because they weren't expecting us. But for now, our suggestion is that we head home where it's safer. You have had an absolutely miserable day, and it looks like you need some rest."

An evil, interdimensional creature with an unfathomable number of minds is concerned about me. My life has gotten very weird.

"And me?" Yuriel asked from a dozen feet away. "Sorry if I don't exactly trust you right now."

"Oh, that's fine. Doesn't change the fact that you're coming with us." Rafe chuckled. "We're not letting you out of our sight."

"Do I have a say in the matter?" Yuriel put his hand on his gun, now back in his holster.

"Absolutely not." Rafe grinned wide, a feral expression that was entirely unlike the stoic and stern professor. "Wanna fight about it? That would be a great deal of fun. We've never danced with a Host before."

Yuriel watched him narrowly. "I'd rather not."

"We would just destroy you now, eat you whole. It's the smart choice, and we all know it. But *somebody* would get upset." Rafe hugged her tight to his side. "And we can't have that."

"I'm right here." She pushed on his chest, but he didn't budge. "And will you please let—will you please let Rafe drive again? You're a little—um—unnerving."

He laughed mirthfully. At least he wasn't offended. The things in charge of Rafe's body smiled down at her with real fondness on their borrowed features. He cradled her head in his hand before leaning down to kiss her, tender and soft. When he broke away, he moved his head to her ear and whispered. "You'll get used to it. In fact...we expect you'll learn to *love* it."

The innuendo was clear.

Even before he grabbed her ass.

She smacked him hard on the chest.

He pulled away, laughing as he did. "Fine, fine. We won't have any fun at all. Very well." Rafe took in a breath, shut his eyes, straightened his shoulders...and promptly collapsed.

"Rafe!" Emma tried to catch him. Unfortunately, he was twice her size and took her easily down to the ground. But she did manage to keep his head from bouncing off the pavement, so she took that as a win.

The man in question groaned, turned onto his side, and promptly retched. What came out of his mouth was...it looked like hot tar. Black, viscous, and oddly lumpy.

Yuriel wrinkled his nose. "That...would be what was left of the Idol's Crawling Terror."

Rafe mumbled something unintelligible as he wiped his sleeve across his mouth.

Emma furrowed her brow. Well, there went Jim. Some part of her felt weirdly bad for the thing. She had named it, after all. She stroked Rafe's hair gently as he lay there on his side and tried to catch his breath and recover from what had just happened.

When Rafe sought her hand, she smiled despite the situation. He squeezed her hand gently, and she returned the gesture, trying to reassure him that she was there. That everything would be okay. And that whatever he'd become—because of *her*—she wouldn't leave his side.

This was her fault. All of it.

Letting out a long breath, she looked up at Yuriel. "Can you help me get him home?"

"Nothing better to do." He smirked, the sarcasm obvious. "Can you stand, professor?"

"I...believe so." The poor man was shivering. Whatever had happened had put him through the wringer. She helped him stand as best as she could, supporting his weight. But as he nearly toppled over, Yuriel had to catch him. Rafe grunted. "Perhaps not."

Yuriel chuckled and slung the professor's arm over his shoulder. "C'mon, Mirror. Let's get you into a shower and then to bed."

The walk back to Rafe's brownstone was spent largely in silence. Emma trailed along just behind the two men, not knowing quite what to do with herself. She watched Rafe and Yuriel. Each time she looked at the Host, she felt pain. He wore the face of her brother. He wore the *body* of her twin.

But Elliot was dead.

Elliot was gone.

It wasn't Yuriel's fault. He was just some poor...something, caught up in the middle of whatever he had been summoned into—into the Idol's goal of attempting to end the world. And Rafe had wanted nothing to do with any of this. But she had dragged him into it, kicking and screaming.

Now the plan was to sit tight, lay low, and...wait. And do nothing. And wonder every time there was a knock at the door whether it was the postman or some terrible and twisted freak who had come to take her and Yuriel away.

That wasn't sustainable. She didn't know how any of this ended, but it wasn't with her hiding under the blankets waiting for the danger to pass.

"So, we're going to just sit there and do nothing? I don't know how long I'll be able to sit cooped up in Rafe's house," she muttered just loud enough for them to hear. "I'm going to warn you both, I don't *do nothing* very well."

"No shit," Yuriel said.

"You're kidding," Rafe said at the same time.

"Har har." She rolled her eyes, tucking her hands into her pockets and jogging to catch up to walk beside the two men. They had longer legs, and even with Rafe's slower pace, they walked faster than she did. "I mean it. We can't just…wait."

"I know." Rafe let out a breath. "But the Bishop wants to act first. And I do not like the idea of being dragged off by his Investigators or hanged for blasphemy. He picks the next move. Not us."

Yuriel said something under his breath to Rafe, something she wasn't meant to hear. It was a question.

Rafe replied with a tired sound and a shake of his head.

"What?" She frowned. "What did you ask him?"

"Nothing," Yuriel lied.

"No. No, I'm fucking *done* with that. Enough secrets. What did you just ask him?" Emma had half a mind to point her pistol at him. But she figured she had enough enemies; she didn't need to make one out of the body of her twin being driven about by a creature who was either an angel or a demon.

Rafe and Yuriel shared a glance. Rafe shrugged.

Yuriel sighed. "I asked him if he was a Saint now."

"A what?" She blinked. "I mean, I know what a Saint is, but…"

"When we become too dangerous—when any of us become too in tune with the Great Beast, and our power ascends to a certain level," Rafe took over the task of explaining it to her, "we are dubbed a Saint."

"Like Gigi?"

"No. You can rule a cult and not be a Saint." Rafe paused. "And no Saint has ever existed for more than a few weeks before the Church deals with them by any means necessary. It's a death wish."

"I wanted to know if we were in real danger," Yuriel added.

"Then why become a Saint at all? Why take the risk?" It made no sense to her.

Rafe's expression went thin as he glared at the street ahead of them. "Because sometimes you don't have a choice."

The implication was clear.

She'd shot him. She'd ruined the ward he had on his back, giving the Things that occupied him the opportunity to take more control.

She went quiet for a moment before she finally answered. "Oh."

"Yes, *oh.*" Rafe sighed. "No, I am not yet a Saint. The Bishop and I had a conversation, and he would have known what I was if I had been corrupted to that level. But I don't know if that path is inevitable for me now or not. I don't know if the disease will metastasize or if it's stable. If it's…" He glanced at her. "Content."

Her cheeks went a little warm.

Rafe smiled, just the barest hint of warmth on otherwise stern features. "The Bishop claims I've corrupted the darkness just as much as it has corrupted me. Perhaps that's true after all."

She didn't know what to say to that.

Yuriel squinted at the professor. "Was that you trying to flirt? Because that was terrible." He made a *gleh* noise. "Hey, sweetheart, I'm so into you that the darkness that wants to gorge itself on meat is totally fine fucking you instead." Yuriel hummed. "I mean, you are a wonderful piece of ass, I'll give them that."

Emma wailed. "Don't say that!"

"What?" Yuriel snickered. "It's true, isn't it?"

"I don't need you talking about me that way. You're—okay, you're not my brother, but you're close enough, and I don't—ew!" She waved her arms in front of herself, as if trying to wipe something off.

Yuriel cackled. "Fine, I won't say it."

"Thank you," she replied.

"Even if it is true." He grinned.

"Augh!" Emma covered her face with her hands. "Just stop." When she looked up, Yuriel was grinning like an idiot. And Rafe had the look of a man who was praying to be struck by lightning to put him out of his misery.

Luckily, it wasn't long before they made it back to his home. The house was quiet as they walked in, with nobody except Hector sitting on the stairs, glaring at them all, her tail swishing quietly beside her.

"I'll take up a spare room. You kids have a great night." Yuriel walked away from them and headed off into the house, leaving Rafe leaning on the stairway railing. "Try not to keep me up, eh?"

"Please shut up." Emma whined.

By that time, Rafe could walk a little easier, and she could help him take a quick shower and change into clothes that weren't soaked with sweat. He almost collapsed into his bed. Sitting on the edge of the bed, she leaned down to kiss him.

He sought her hand again, squeezing it. "Stay with me," he murmured as she broke the kiss. "Sleep here tonight."

"Do you think that's a good idea?" She frowned. "What with...y'know. *Them* and all."

"They're fed and...amused. They'll be quiet tonight." He

let out a breath. "I don't want to be alone, even though I just...there are so many voices. I don't know how to explain it. I—" He cringed.

Her heart broke. God above, below, or whoever, she didn't care who was listening, she prayed to them for an ounce of pity for the professor. "You don't need to." Stroking his hair, she smiled sadly. "Trust me, I understand."

"Emma! Please, please, it's the only thing that makes it stop. I can't explain it." The voice of her brother beside her rang out like he was standing there. She knew that time it was a memory. She had once found Elliot sitting in the bathroom, a razor in his hands, having sliced up his arms and legs. The pain had made the voices quieter.

Pain, and drugs, and...Elliot would have given anything for some silence. And it turns out in the end, he did.

Leaning down, she kissed Rafe again. "Let me change. I'll be right back. I promise."

He nodded, his dark eyes slipping shut. The poor man was exhausted. She left him to go change into her nightgown, and when she came back, he was already quietly snoring in the bed, Hector curled up by his knees.

The lines on his face were smooth. He looked at peace. But there on the wall, right beside her, in the shadow cast by the moonlight hitting a sconce on the wall, was a tendril of darkness that was lazily curling and flexing.

"Hi," she whispered. She reached out and gently placed her hand on the wall. The tendril responded immediately, wrapping itself around her wrist and curling through her fingers. It was holding her hand in the same way Rafe had just been doing.

It—they? *This is extremely confusing.* Whatever. The tendril wasn't being aggressive. It wasn't even being possessive. She could pull her hand away if she needed to. Rafe's shadowy monsters had saved her. Protected her. Had defeated the Idol's monsters to keep her safe.

She didn't really understand why. Because Rafe wanted her safe as he'd insinuated, maybe? Or maybe it was something more. She smiled at the tendril and kept her voice to a whisper. "Thank you."

The tendril squeezed her fingers briefly before it released her and disappeared back into the darkness. She slipped underneath the covers and snuggled up next to Rafe. He muttered something in his sleep and reached out for her. She hugged his arm and rested her head close to his on the pillow.

It had been a long day.

A very long few days.

Sleep came for her hard and fast.

CHAPTER NINETEEN

Patrick had made a terrible mistake.

He had plenty of crosses. He didn't *need* to go backstage to confront Gigi and get that one back. Yes, fine, it had belonged to his family. Yes, fine, it was somewhat sentimental to him.

But he had others.

And this was a very, very bad idea.

When he stepped into Gigi's dressing room, he felt as though he had stepped into the jaws of the hells themselves. And if there was ever a succubus who had come to lure him into his damnation, it was the one that lay sprawled out on her chaise lounge, casually smoking a cigarette, and toying with *his* necklace that she wore.

Shit, shit, shit, shit—

"Hello, priest." Gigi smiled coyly at him. She was naked beneath the layers of her chiffon nightgown. He couldn't see the details, but he could see enough as she bent a knee through the part, baring her leg. She had a white fur pelt draped over her torso, hiding the parts that he knew he wouldn't be able to help but stare at. Not like it was stopping him from trying. "Did you enjoy the show?"

Shit, shit, shit, shit! "I would like to have my cross back, thank you." It took everything in him to keep his voice from cracking or sounding far huskier than he wanted it to. As Gigi stared at him with one thin eyebrow raised, he cringed. "The show was lovely."

"Mmhm." Gigi wrapped the chain of his cross around her fingers, winding and unwinding it. "I thought perhaps we could take this opportunity to get to know each other better, priest." She gestured at the drinks on the table beside him.

"I should just take my cross and go." He tightened his hands into fists at his sides. Damn it all, he meant to sound intimidating. Instead, he sounded as unsure as he felt.

Gigi smiled coquettishly, reclining farther back into the cushions and the fur pelt. "Oh, sweetheart…*should* isn't a word that carries a lot of weight around here."

"That is, in fact, part of the problem." He sighed. "I'm not staying."

"Come, now, just a drink and a chat. You're here to learn how to manipulate me into doing what you want, aren't you?" She stretched one arm over her head, arching her back. The fur covered the front of her breasts, but not the side.

Patrick had to shut his eyes and look away. By the Benevolent God, how he wanted her. How he wanted to taste her, to feel her. This was sin. Sin and temptation. "This isn't about manipulation."

"Sure, it isn't. We're both in this for the same reason, priest. We want to make sure the Idol doesn't get what they want. We want to keep that silly Mather girl safe. And…right now? You and I are both looking at each other like a wonderful opportunity."

"Oh?" He kept his gaze firmly planted on a spot on the wall.

"You want to control me and, ergo, my society of *friends*." She chuckled. "And I want to be safe from you and your little white-masked freaks. I have no interest in being hanged by the neck until dead, or burned at the stake, or whatever it is you do to people you deem heretics."

He had no comment on that.

Gigi continued. "Here, we have an opportunity to achieve both those things...and enjoy each other's company. Why not take a little pleasure in our work?"

"I should not be associating with you. This whole scheme was a mistake. You're..."

"Pah. I'm what?" Gigi pulled from her cigarette and let out a long curl of smoke, speaking as she exhaled. "I've never once taken a life, you know."

He scoffed. "I find that hard to believe."

"You don't know anything about us, priest. Your Church stamps us out, drives us into the darkness." Her voice went cold, her flirtatiousness instantly gone. "The Blade asks for nothing that is not willingly sacrificed. We don't take lives. We don't *need* to. But I don't blame you for assuming otherwise." She shrugged. "What with all the serial killers running amok in this city like that bastard professor, and all."

"Tell me you aren't lying to me." That time he sought out her gaze.

She was watching him with a faint smile, one that actually seemed...genuine. For all her flash, and all her pomp, and how beautiful she was with all the glitz and glamor, he found that faint smile drove deeper into him than anything else.

When she spoke, her voice was calm. Sincere. "I'm generally not a liar, priest. I don't make a practice of it unless I have to. I haven't fibbed to you since we met." She hummed. "You've got that kind of face, I suppose. Pulls the honesty out of everyone, doesn't it?"

"That or my fists."

Her laugh was joyful, and she watched him, a little shocked and yet surprised. "My, my, priest. Now you're starting to bite back. I like it." She shifted on the chaise lounge, turning onto her side, the fur covering threatening to slide loose. "Well, if you're going to bend me over your knee to get a confession from me, I just ask you to use an open palm instead, if you must. And...nowhere that'll show on stage, hm?" She winked. "The show must go on, after all."

His face, if it hadn't already been, must now be the color of a tomato with how hot his cheeks felt. No matter how hard he tried, he couldn't help but picture it. Her pale, beautiful ass in the air as he turned it a shade of pink with the strike of his hand. Her, whimpering and begging for mercy. And for more.

Shit, shit, shit.

"Have a seat, priest. Before you pass out from all the blood rushing to your head. And...elsewhere." She smirked and took another drag from her cigarette. "I promise I'll be a good girl."

The sound that left him was half of what wanted to break loose. He was staring at the spider. He had walked into her web. He was two steps away from freedom. He could turn, leave, and she couldn't stop him.

His feet moved. But not toward the door.

GIGI WATCHED as Bishop Patrick Caner sat down in the chair across from her table, looking stiff as a board in more ways than one. His cassock did a decent job of hiding his arousal, but from the looks of things, it had a lot to obscure. *Goodness, I do hope he's to scale.* She wondered if he was a violent lover, secretly hiding the need to dominate his partners. Or if he was more considerate. Or passive.

She could see it going any which way with the priest. Perhaps he wanted her to ride him, to pretend he wasn't an active participant. Perhaps he wanted to worship her. Perhaps he wanted to control her. If she was lucky, she'd get to try all the flavors he had to offer.

Oh, no, Gigi. What're you doing? Don't go getting attached. Even if the look on his face when he dropped his guard was so wonderful. Usually, he was just glaring at her, trying to put up a big show. But when he softened at the edges, when he put away his distaste for the dark arts and was just a man...he was beautiful.

She gestured to the drinks on the table. Letting out a breath, Patrick went straight for the bottle of whiskey and poured a great deal more into his glass.

Gigi laughed again, folding her arms on the side of the chaise lounge to rest her chin on them. "I suppose you are a big man. You probably need a lot to get you cozy."

"Being Irish doesn't help." He gulped down the entire glass of alcohol and went back to the bottle like it had been apple juice instead. "Hope you don't mind if I empty this."

"Not in the slightest." She couldn't help but be curious about him. "What brought you here, priest?"

"I've had family out here in Arnsmouth for ages, all members of the Church. I came here when I was little more than a boy, and I decided I wanted to join." He shook his head. "Pretty soon it was clear that I have a particular touch for...rooting out the Dark Societies, you could say."

"You mean you have a particular touch for violence." She huffed. She knew the stories.

"Yeah. Family has also been boxers for generations." He chuckled and scratched at his stubble. She wanted to know how it would feel against her skin. He kept talking. "I suppose I'm a bit of a mix of the two. I try not to knock heads around if I don't have to."

"How many men have you killed?" She reached for her own glass and sipped the bitter alcohol. But she wasn't about to let Patrick put the bottle down without her having some. "And women, I suppose."

"No more than I've had to, like I said." He frowned. "And I don't enjoy a damn second of any of it."

Gigi tilted her head thoughtfully. It wasn't a very flirtatious question, but she had always wanted to know. Now it seemed like it might be the only chance she might get. "Where do they go? The ones who ascend to Sainthood?"

He grimaced. "They aren't Saints."

"That's what we call them."

"And they aren't Saints." There was that hard look on his face again. She'd pulled the curtain back down.

"All right, suit yourself. Okay, the *powerful* ones. Where do they go? What do you do with them?" She sipped her drink. "I've always been so curious."

"They're dealt with." He paused, and she watched his expression fall. "I can't say, Gigi. There are things I can't tell you."

"That's all right. I have plenty of secrets of my own." She smiled. "I just had to ask."

Patrick's second glass of whiskey was already half gone. He watched her, just as she watched him. Curious, wary, distrustful.

Wanting.

A want that had not yet become a need. But it would. She made sure to shift the fur stole just a little to the left, almost revealing one of her nipples, but not quite.

His eyes traveled the length of her body. "Why're you playing this game with me?"

"Game?" She feigned innocence. "I just like to relax after a performance, that's all."

He dropped his head, rubbing his hand over his brow. "I'm not an idiot, Gigi."

"Fine." She chuckled, unable to help it. "I know, but you're so adorable when you're flustered. You're so much fun to tease."

"I wish you wouldn't."

"And I think that's not true." When he shot her a look, she smiled and leaned back once more, stretching her legs out over the length of the lounge. "You're here specifically because you like to be teased, I think. No one else dares to do this with you, do they? No, they either worship at your feet or they run in terror…"

Opening his mouth, he went to argue, and then stopped. Bless his heart, he really was an open book. He sighed and finished the rest of his glass. "Fair."

A man who was willing to admit when he was beat. *Be still, my heart.* She decided it was time to roll the dice. Slowly, making sure he saw every single movement, she stood, keeping the fur draped over her body.

His eyes went wide as she approached him. She took every step with all the confidence in the world, her head held high. She wasn't a parishioner. She wasn't penitent. Nor would she cower. She was who she was. And he was the Bishop who had vanished dozens of her compatriots, admittedly killing them or bringing them somewhere he couldn't say.

This was a dangerous game for both of them.

But those were the best ones to play.

PATRICK'S BREATH caught in his chest as Gigi stood from the lounge. The chiffon did little to hide her body in the light, and the fur only barely hid her nakedness. She walked up to him like a lioness, and he wasn't certain if he was a fellow lion or a gazelle.

He didn't know which he wanted to be.

Both, perhaps.

When she stood in front of him, he didn't know what to do. He stared at her, eyes wide, frozen. She didn't seem to mind. She placed her hand on his shoulder and gently urged him to lean back in the chair.

"I—" he tried.

She placed a finger to his lips. "Shush."

Benevolent God, help me. Save me.

Forgive me.

Gigi straddled his legs, the chiffon gown parting on the side as she shifted before sitting down on his thighs. She barely weighed a thing—he was probably nearly triple her weight. But the warmth of her, the presence of her...the smell of flowers, mixing with the tang of smoke and whiskey.

Her hand trailed over his features, tracing his jawline, brushing against his stubble, before slipping through his short hair, her long nails grazing his scalp.

It was all he could do to bite back a groan. She smiled, sinful and sweet, and leaned in close to his lips. "I want you, Bishop Patrick Caner. I want you very badly."

"You just want to"—he almost choked when she shifted her hips on his thighs, sliding closer to him—"control me."

"A mutually...beneficial partnership...that's what this is." She traced a nail over his lower lip. "But this doesn't have to be *all* business, does it?"

"It's manipulation. You're just using me for—" He was silenced once more with a finger.

"I could. But I'm not." Her eyes were dark and lidded with lust. "I don't fuck for power. That's a promise I made to myself a long time ago. This isn't part of our negotiations. This is just us. Understand?"

"Just us." He repeated it, his voice sounding like it had been rolled in gravel. Demons had possessed him. That was the only excuse he could think of. He nodded.

And she kissed him.

HE SMELLED of cologne and tasted like whiskey. His lips were so firm against hers—he was like a chiseled block of stone. By the Great Beast, he was glorious. He was absolutely, undoubtedly perfect.

She deepened the kiss as she cradled the back of his head, not letting him escape. With her other hand, she began to deftly undo the buttons of his cassock, starting at his neck and slowly trailing downward.

I'm going to fuck the Bishop of the Church of the Benevolent God.

It was so ludicrous it almost made her laugh. She wondered if he'd fight her, slap her hand away, or break the kiss to insist he was a holy man, and he was above her. *I want him above me. And below me. And I want to be the naughty girl he forces to confess. I want to kneel and worship him. I want him to pray at* my *altar.*

Shit, if she wasn't careful, she really was going to get attached.

His hands finally moved, but not to push her away. They settled on her thighs, heavy and large, and squeezed her legs tentatively, as if exploring the action. As if he wasn't sure he was allowed to touch her.

She wouldn't be that mean.

When the buttons of his cassock were undone, she split the fabric to trail her hands over his shirt, feeling the expansive muscles underneath. He was *huge,* and he was built like a truck. She loved how the cords of muscle rippled beneath her hands as she slid them along his sides, stroking over him. Exploring him. Urging him to do the same.

He groaned against her lips, a rumble that went through her like thunder. Oh, yes. The desire was very much mutual between them. She began to undo his shirt buttons the same as she had his cassock, if far more impatiently.

When her hands reached his belt, she finally broke the kiss to lean back and watch him. His green eyes were almost blackened emeralds as he took her in.

She trailed her hand lower, slipping between his legs, and cupped the bulge that had been desperately begging for freedom since she stepped foot onto the stage earlier that night.

He hissed air sharply in through his nose. The vein in his neck was pulsing. When she squeezed, his eyes slipped shut and another low moan left him.

So beautiful.

It didn't take much work to free him from his trousers, though he needed to help her scoot his pants down a little to truly let his full glory out into the open.

It was her turn to moan.

Oh, he *was* to scale to the rest of him. She placed one hand against his shoulder, resting against the side of his neck, his shirt parted and pushed aside. And with her other hand, she grasped his length—her fingers couldn't reach all the way around—and began to stroke him.

The shudder that went through him was blissful to watch. His lips parted as he shut his eyes, clearly struggling with the sensations.

He was volcanic to the touch and hard as a damnable rock like the rest of him. She really had pushed him to the edge, she could tell. Poor bastard. She had wanted to simply suck him off the first time they played together—give him a taste of what he could have and make sure she lured him back for more.

But now that she saw him? Felt him? Tasted him? Damn it all, she was going to be selfish. She wanted to feel *all* of him. She patiently stroked him, firm and slow, as she sought his lips with hers again, this time teasing with the tip of her tongue, asking for entry.

He parted and let her in, his tongue twisting with hers as he met her passion in kind. His hands roamed her—*finally!*—and left their perch on her thighs to wander her back and her sides. But damn it if he wasn't far too polite for her tastes.

She'd have to force the issue, wouldn't she?

When they parted from the kiss, they were both breathless, though he was far more so than she. He had begun to thrust his hips up into her hand, little more than a reflexive press of his muscles.

Leaning back from him, she finally let go of his length, though she was honestly sad to do so. She made sure he was watching her as she pulled the fur stole from her shoulder and dropped it to the ground. His gaze dropped to her body, now barely concealed beneath the chiffon gown.

She took both his hands in hers, keeping his palms flat to her body as she laced her fingers with his much larger ones. She guided him to the drawstring of her gown. "Go on, priest…"

All the air left his lungs as he carefully undid the tie before slipping his fingers underneath the hem at her shoulders and gently pushing it from her. Soon, it was a puddle on the ground, and she was naked before him.

It was then she had her answer as to what kind of lover the Bishop was.

It was as if a gun had gone off at the races. Like the crack of a whip that drove the herd forward into a stampede.

A growl left him, low and guttural. He placed a hand

against her back, the stretch of his fingers almost as wide as she was, the other hand suddenly grasping her hip tight enough she wondered if she might bruise.

He leaned her back, lowering his head to her chest, and attacked her breast with his mouth as if he was a starving man at a feast. Gigi gasped, wrapping her arms around him and holding on, afraid she might fall backward. But she had no reason to worry—he was as strong as an ox.

Tongue rolling over her pert bud, he moaned against her skin and pulled her hips closer to his, his length rubbing up against her.

She rocked her hips, grinding herself against that hard length, seeking the friction against her sensitive bud of nerves. "Yes, oh—yes, priest—"

"Bishop," he muttered against her skin.

She grinned. "No. I think I like 'priest' better."

He bit her, his teeth sharp against her sensitive nipple.

She gasped and moaned, arching into it. "Oh, if that's you punishing me, I'll have to act up more."

"Not sure if you can get much worse." He kissed her chest between her breasts.

"Don't threaten me with a good time. I—" She squealed as he stood up. She wrapped her legs around his waist, shocked at the movement. He walked them both to her lounge, carrying her like she weighed nothing, before gently placing her down on the lounge on her back.

He kneeled between her legs, looking down at her as if in awe. "Gigi…"

She stroked a hand over his stomach, marveling at his perfect body, still hidden under his clothes. "I want to see you. All of you."

There was no hesitation in him as he shrugged out of his clothes, tossing his shirt, undershirt, and cassock aside. The rest went a moment later, and she watched each movement in eager anticipation.

He was built like a truck. All muscles, all man, and all *hers*. She was going to get a lot of mileage out of the tires on that particular vehicle. When he returned to her, he surprised her yet again.

He bent his head to her and began to kiss his way down her body, lingering at her breasts, toying with her nipples once more before traveling lower. Slow, sultry kisses traced a line down, and down, and—

"Ooh, Bishop—"

She'd concede that one. He earned it. He hooked one of her legs over his shoulder as his tongue lavished her core, knowing just where to go. Just where to tease. Each time she twitched or gasped, he focused on that spot. He was a quick learner—more importantly, he *wanted* to learn. There was nothing more valuable in the world than an intuitive lover.

A finger slipped inside her, broad, and thick, and she arched her back, biting back a wail. He slowly pressed his finger as far as the knuckle before drawing back, repeating the action slowly, again, and again.

He was watching her now as he slipped a second finger inside. She writhed, whimpering as he stretched her. He was preparing her for the girth of him—oh, bless his sweet heart. While she loved a rough ride, she wouldn't say no to some careful foreplay. It was so rare.

But a girl only had so much patience. "Patrick…I need you," she gasped. Oh, he was good. Very good.

He slid his way up her body, her leg sliding down to hook her knee over his elbow. It spread her wide, her other thigh resting on his as he balanced his weight over her. She felt him there, at her core, throbbing and wonderful. "I don't want to hurt you," he murmured.

"You won't." She ran her hands over his bare chest and

found it just as wonderful as she had hoped. "Trust me. Now...fuck me, priest. Fuck me like you mean it."

And he did just as she told him.

By the God above and the Beast below, she felt impossible. She was a vise around him, hot as lava, and the way she moved as he plunged himself into her depths almost ended him right then and there.

When he finally had himself buried to the hilt, she was gasping and crying out in pleasure, whispering his name, and begging him for more. He leaned some of his weight on her and felt her spasm around him, tightening even farther, her pleasure peaking into ecstasy. And yet again, she almost dragged him over that edge with her.

She wrapped her other leg around his waist, trying to pull him in closer. Trying to get more out of him. "Harder—"

Gigi Gage was going to be the death of him. One way or another. *This is the best possible option, by far.* He drew back his hips and snapped them forward, testing the waters. She bucked with the impact, those perfect breasts of hers bouncing with the thrust.

She tossed her head back, her hand curled by her cheek. "Yes—yes—harder!"

Far be it from him to refuse a lady.

Gigi hadn't been fucked so well in *years.*

Damn the ox analogy, he was a damnable stallion. He rutted her like a machine, like a man unhinged, using all his weight and all his power to stretch her, fill her, to threaten her control. To send her into bliss enough times she couldn't think straight.

He was almost too much for her to take, and it was the best kind of ache when he drove himself home. But he was only human—sadly—and both of them were sweating, panting, and past the point of no return.

"Once more," she murmured between gasps. "Once more, priest. Stop holding back." She grinned. "I can take it."

Growling, he threw her other leg up over his other arm, nearly folding her in half, and that time the thrust inside her felt like it had gone into her damn lungs. She couldn't speak anymore as he rampaged inside her, rutting her like a man possessed.

It sent her into ecstasy again, her climax grasping what was left of her mind and throwing it out the window. It was enough to end him, and he clutched her close, dropping her legs so she could wrap them around his waist as he surged inside her, letting out a broken-sounding moan into the pillow beside her head.

The feeling of him flooding her sent her already peaked pleasure to a new high. *Yes, yes, yes!* She held him as close as she could, feeling the sweat of his body against her as he twitched, each motion spending more of him inside her.

Defile me, priest.

I want it all.

He collapsed onto his elbows, gasping and panting, and let out a quiet, pathetic whimper. It had her chuckling; it was so adorable. Scratching at his scalp at the base of his neck, she kissed his cheek, urging him to turn to her.

Obeying, he kissed her, slowly and tenderly, before they both couldn't spare the air anymore and had to break away. When he could breathe, he muttered, "I want my necklace back."

She put on her best fake pout. "But I'm fond of it."

"No."

Sighing, she took it off and slipped it around his neck. "You're no fun at all."

"Right." He smirked briefly before his expression fell. "I..."

"Shush." She kissed him again slowly, enjoying the shape of his lips against hers. "You and I are business partners. And now, we're also lovers. Now...we both need a shower, and you're going to go out the back like nothing happened. Sound good?"

"I'm new to this whole...casual lovers thing."

"You're in good hands." She grinned.

"I noticed." It was his turn to shoot her a cheeky smile for once.

Laughing, she nudged him away from her. "Off, stallion. Showering is required now."

"Stallion?" He sat back on the chaise lounge before reaching for the whiskey and pouring himself another glass and downing it in one go. "I've been promoted."

"You earned it." She gestured toward a door by the wall. "You first."

"Ladies go first."

"But if you're sweaty and naked when someone walks in, it's conspicuous. For me, it's normal." She chuckled. "Go on."

Patrick grunted as he got up to walk away, gathering his clothes as he went. It afforded her a wonderful view of his ass. It was just as muscular as the rest of him, and she enjoyed the view the entire time.

When he finally left the room, muttering complaints the whole way, she chuckled and pulled one of her blankets over her. She felt triumphant. She felt glorious. But there was something else there that was surprising, and as welcome as it was dangerous.

She was happy.

The Bishop made her *happy.*

And that was the deadliest kind of drug.

I'll just have to get rid of him before I get too close, that's all. Besides, something was going to go terribly wrong, long before that ever had a chance to happen. That was just the way of her life.

Shutting her eyes, she let herself doze for a little while the Bishop was showering. As if she had summoned chaos with the simple thought, her suspicion turned into truth in the snap of a finger.

Or in the firing of a gun.

And the sounds of screams.

"Gigi Gage!" someone shouted from inside her club. And she knew that voice. *"You are to come forward immediately!"*

Dr. Thaddeus Kirkbride.

Her whole body went cold as if she had jumped into a freezing bath. She scrambled for her clothing, her movements instinctual. Dr. Thaddeus Kirkbride was here! *No, no, no! Shit!*

The Candle had come.

And where the Dark Society of the Candle went…death and torment followed.

CHAPTER TWENTY

Emma woke up to the feeling of someone twisting a lock of her hair around their fingers, slowly toying with the strand. Her hair was curly, so it just begged to be tangled. She understood. Smiling, she stretched and yawned, nuzzling into the man lying on his back beside her.

"Did I wake you?" Rafe murmured.

"No. But it's a great way to wake up all the same."

He kissed the top of her head, and she let out a contented sigh. The Idol was coming for them. But at least…at least there was this. "Are you all right?" She almost didn't want to ask. It was a stupid question.

"No." At least he was honest. "And I don't believe I ever will be again." Maybe a little too honest.

She pushed up onto her elbows, watching him with a frown. His eyes were shut, and although his voice didn't give much away, she could see the sadness tinging his expression. Reaching out, she stroked his hair gently. "Do you want to talk about it?"

"What is there to talk about?" He laughed sarcastically. "I am now possessed by the countless, nameless, shifting void itself. To know them is to know an unfathomable madness. I hear them whispering to me in a language I *shouldn't* understand. One that if spoken aloud would unravel the very nature of our reality." He opened his eyes to look at her. "They are endless. They are untold. And they are nothing, all at once. And now...I am them. A legion of emptiness. So, never mind. Yes, Emma. I'm perfectly fine."

She laughed, though she knew that probably wasn't the right response. "I'm sorry I asked." She leaned in, kissing his cheek, before snuggling closer to him. "I don't know exactly how to respond to that. Except, well, I'm sorry for shooting you."

"If you hadn't, you would be the prisoner of the Idol now. You would be gone, same as your brother." He sighed. "It has its uses. I'm simply glad *They* don't seem to want to harm you."

"I'm not shocked."

"Hum?"

"Your cat." She smiled faintly. "They never ate your cat, did they? And she's a cat. All she does is find dark corners to sit in."

"Well..." He paused. "Yes, but..." He paused again. "Huh. I suppose I never realized that."

"Not so smart now, are you, professor?" She snickered quietly.

He playfully nudged her. "Be nice. I'm having a terrible week."

She smiled. "Fine, fine."

They lay there quietly for a moment before he spoke up. "But, to your point, I hadn't realized that they avoided Hector. They have corrupted me, but I have corrupted them in turn, it seems. Or filtered them, perhaps."

"They want to do terrible things to me because *you* want

to do terrible things to me?" She lifted her head to smirk at him. "I see. So, you're to blame."

"I didn't hear you complaining." He smirked back at her, his hand trailing down her body to grab one of her ass cheeks, and none too gently at that.

She hissed in pain and slid closer to him to avoid his grasp, not that it worked. And not that she really minded. "I guess we have to be quiet now that Yuriel is in the house."

"He isn't."

She blinked, frowning down at him. "What?"

"He's gone." Rafe shut his eyes. "He left in the night."

"How do you kn—" She sighed. Right. Them. "Never mind. Why?" She fought the urge to say they needed to go after him. Yuriel was a grown man, or demon, or angel, or whatever, and it was his choice to go where he pleased. She wasn't his keeper.

"He left a note, I think." Rafe shrugged. "But I expect it's because you are in more danger when you're together than apart. The Idol has to split their efforts to capture you if you're separated. And it might have something to do with the fact that I was going to kill him."

"Excuse me?" She said that a little louder than she intended.

When he reopened his eyes, they were a little darker than before, as though ink was trying to seep into them at the edges. "Correction—*we* were going to kill him. It was only a matter of time."

She couldn't repress the shudder that ran through her. "But—"

"The protections we afford you don't apply to everyone, simply because you want them to." He grinned. "And no, not even if you asked very, very nicely." His hand was on her ass again, squeezing.

"Point made, but—" She squirmed. "Maybe not right now?"

He arched an eyebrow. "Why not? We're supposed to be 'laying low,' aren't we? How else are we supposed to pass the time?"

"I—" To say she was confused would be putting it lightly. He was terrifying. She should be running and screaming in fear. But instead, as always, her response to dangerous situations only served to light the fire in her, making her want to provoke him into being *worse*. She wanted to see him at his most terrifying.

She wanted the monster in him.

I am incredibly problematic.

When something wrapped around her ankle, thick as a boa constrictor and just as strong, squeezing as it began to worm its way higher to her calf, she let out a wavering breath, her eyes sliding shut.

"That's it, pretty girl..." His voice became a low rumble, almost a purr, as he reached up to stroke her cheek. "Last time was only a sample of what we can do to you. Are you ready for a little bit more? We'll take it nice and slow...ish."

They should be going after Yuriel, or trying to help Patrick, or setting up protections against the Idol, or—

His hand tightened on her ass again, squeezing harder, digging his fingers into her flesh. It pulled a moan out of her, emptying her head of the thoughts of what they should be doing.

She was saved by the bell.

Namely, the doorbell.

The sound Rafe made was one of pure and unadulterated rage. But as the chime of the bell rang again, the growl turned into a deep sigh. "We'll continue this in a moment."

The tendril around her ankle unwrapped itself as he slipped out from under her. He quickly got dressed and was pulling his suspenders over his shoulders as the bell rang a third time. "Yes, yes. We're coming!" His voice lowered to a grumble. "We have a damn mail slot."

Emma couldn't help but chuckle.

"What?" He shot her a look.

"Ancient and unknowable, unfathomable creatures of the madness of the void…inconvenienced by a doorbell." She sat up, running her hands through her hair, trying to tame the wild curls. "It's funny, is all."

"Being focused through a human body has its pros and cons, we'll admit." He shrugged. "But we get your point."

"You might want to put Them away before you answer the door. No need to terrify whoever's there." She went to get dressed herself, but it was going to take her longer than Rafe. Women's clothes weren't exactly speedy, what with the stockings and the garters and the rest of her underthings.

"I suppose." Rafe headed out of the room as the bell rang a fourth time. "Yes, yes! Patience."

The line between the professor and the monster was clearly becoming more and more blurred as time went on. She wondered how long it would be before there wasn't a line at all. She wondered if she would care when it happened.

She wondered if she'd be alive when it did.

By the time she caught up with him, he was closing the door again, looking down at a letter in his hand.

"Who was it?" She was still trying to comb out her hair.

"No one." He ripped up the message, tearing it into quarters, before tucking it into his pants pocket. "It wasn't important."

That was an absolutely miserable lie if she had ever heard one. She knew better than to call him on it or insist that he tell her what was happening. He'd just refuse. Not like she could force it out of him.

But he'd expect her to at least try. "Are you sure?"

"Very." He waved a hand dismissively. "The Dean is very upset that I've been missing my lectures. It was a sternly worded letter that if I do it again, I'll be fired. I honestly couldn't care less."

That didn't sound like Rafe. The darkness was getting better at calling itself "I" instead of "we," making it even harder to tell when one was in control or the other. Great. Fantastic. With a sigh, she shook her head. "I'm sorry if you get fired."

"It's fine." He smiled. "Not like I need the money."

She blinked. "You're wealthy?"

"Extremely." He leaned down to pet Hector, who was purring and rubbing against his legs. "My connections with the Mirror have their benefits. Brokering secrets is a lucrative trade—either making sure they stay unknown, or making sure they become known, as the case may be."

"Then…why work?" She finished descending the stairs. "Why be a professor?"

"Because some of us have goals in life, Princess. I enjoy it." He smiled teasingly at her. "Or did. I suspect that's over now."

Guilt stabbed at her again. "I've ruined your life, haven't I?"

"Not entirely." He stood from his crouch and walked up to her, that fiendish look slowly creeping back onto his face. "Only mostly."

Her heart leapt into her throat as he approached, the darkness in his eyes growing once more. Taking her chin in his hand, he leaned down to capture her lips in a kiss. It was slow, but searing, making his intentions very well known.

She held on to his waist to keep from losing her balance, letting out a quiet whimper as his hand slid to cradle the back of her neck, threading his fingers into her hair.

This man was going to be the death of her.

Figuratively and literally.

When he broke away, she was shivering. He smiled dangerously. "But I know how you can make it up to me."

"Breakfast first." She gently urged him away. "I'm starving. I'll cook this time. You don't want me passing out on you, do you?" She poked him in the chest.

He tilted his head to the side. "Humans. So needy. All right. Suit yourself."

Turning to head up the stairs to the second-floor kitchen, she called back to him. "I'll let you know when it's ready."

"We'll be down here, coming up with the list of all the things we're going to do to you. The longer you take, the longer the list." It was said as a threat. It sent another shiver down her spine.

God above, God below, she didn't know what to do with that. "Point taken."

She waited until she got into the kitchen to look down at the ripped-up letter she had lifted from his pocket while they had been kissing. She set it down on the counter and arranged the four quarters.

It was handwritten on letterhead, denoting where it came from. Fear gripped the base of her spine and sent her stomach crashing into the pits as she read its point of origin.

Arnsmouth Asylum.

She read the letter quickly, feeling very cold all of a sudden. *No, no, please no...*

"Ms. Emma Mather,

It has come to my attention that you have sought shelter under the roof of one Professor Raphael Saltonstall while in search of your missing twin brother. It is not my place to point out the foolishness of your decision.

Instead, I would like to invite you to meet with me, so that we may discuss two matters I believe will be of some importance to you.

First, that while you may have been led to believe that your brother's current illness is incurable, I can assure you it is not. I wish to speak to you of potential treatments.

Second, the welfare of one 'Gigi Gage,' with whom I believe you are acquainted and who is now within the care of my institution, may be a matter of some concern to you.

While I am sure you will question my sincerity and your safety within the walls of my institution, I give you my word that my intentions are benign. I simply wish to speak to you of your options going forward.

Your friend,
 Dr. Thaddeus Kirkbride"

Oh, no. Oh, no, no, *no*. Panic sent her heart pounding in her ears. Gigi was a prisoner at the asylum, and—

A hand twisted in her hair, pressing her forward until she was doubled over the countertop. "Naughty girl." Rafe chuckled. "Although I should have guessed."

"Let me go!"

"No." He pushed her dress up over her hips, his hand roaming over her ass once more. "I think not."

"We have to—"

"We are going to do *nothing*, Emma. Your brother is gone. Taken by the darkness. His soul has been scattered to nothing but the energy it began as. He cannot be saved. The doctor is lying. And as for Gigi?" He stroked her thigh before squeezing it, leaning his hips into her, groaning low in his throat. "Who cares?"

"She's been a friend to me. She's tried to help us. We need to do the same for her. Who knows what he'll do to her?"

"Only what she deserves. Don't forget what she is, pretty girl. A monster, just like us." He picked her up by her hair, pulling her back against his chest. "Just like you will be soon."

"W—what?"

He chuckled, malice thick in his voice. "Are you honestly surprised? Did you really think we were going to let you go? No, pretty girl…you belong to us now. We'll let these silly little mortal bodies of yours age away, and you can live with the professor, pretending you're just a normal couple in love. But as time takes its toll, we'll consume you. Make you one of us. Just like we did with him. We'll be together, then…always."

"Stop—" She struggled. "No! Let me go. You can't—"

His hand snapped over her mouth, cutting her off. "We can. And we will. But don't worry, you'll live your normal lifespan. We won't take you a moment too soon. So why all the fuss? You didn't honestly believe you were going to some pathetic afterlife, did you?" He laughed.

She bit his hand as hard as she could, instantly tasting blood against her teeth. She had to slam her elbow into his ribs twice before his grasp loosened enough that she could run. She had expected anger from him. To hear him shouting at her to stop. But what she got was worse.

Laughter. Joyful laughter. "This is our favorite game, Emma! And we suspect it's yours, too. Go ahead. You know you won't make it out the door!"

Unfortunately, she knew that was true.

All of it.

But Gigi needed her help.

And damn it if she wasn't going to try.

PATRICK WAS STILL TOWELING off his hair as Gigi burst into the bathroom. He jolted in surprise. "I—"

"Shut up. Get out. Get your things and go."

He would have been hurt, being pushed out the door so quickly, if it weren't for the look of panic and terror on her face. She was pale and looked as though she had seen a ghost. He frowned. "What's wr—"

"Kirkbride is here." Gigi shook her head, gathering up his cassock from the chair and throwing it at him. "He's here for me. Get your things and leave *now*. He can't find you here."

Kirkbride? Patrick grimaced. The doctor of Arnsmouth Asylum had always been of major concern to him. The leader of the Candle, and a dangerous sociopath. But unfortunately, he was a very well connected and very well-funded monster, and it made him hard to "vanish" appropriately.

That, and it wasn't time yet. Kirkbride had yet to become a "Saint." It was a word he hated using for the monstrosities, but he had to admit it had been used enough that it had stuck. "Damn it. Come with me."

"No. If I don't confront him, he'll murder Mykel and everyone else. Or worse." Gigi turned to the mirror, plucking some lipstick out of her bag to paint her lips crimson. Patrick couldn't help but smile, even just a little. She wanted to face the music looking her absolute best. He wouldn't have expected any less.

"I can't just leave, knowing—"

"It doesn't matter!" She whirled on him angrily. "He's here now. And you're outnumbered. He's come with a gaggle of his *freaks,* and you left all yours at home." She jabbed a finger into the middle of his chest. "And if he finds you, he'll kill you. Or worse."

His jaw ticked. "But—"

"Don't get sentimental, priest. This meant nothing. Just because we fucked doesn't mean we're sweethearts! We're enemies using each other for a good time. That's all. Don't forget who and what I am. Now get. Your shit. And go." She stormed out of the room, slamming the door behind her.

She was right. Painfully so.

Shrugging on his cassock, he buttoned it up and, glowering to himself, found the back exit of the club and left. The streets were empty, and he was glad for it. He knew what Kirkbride did to his so-called patients. He didn't have the desire to fight them off.

Gigi was right. Or rather, she should have been right.

They were enemies. This was just a fight between cults. He should be happy for it—maybe it would thin their ranks a little.

But it felt wrong to abandon her.

Very, very wrong.

Don't get sentimental, priest.

CHAPTER TWENTY-ONE

Gigi kept her head held high as she walked out into her club. It was in total disarray—chairs were everywhere. Tables were flipped. Several of her people were dead, lying in puddles of their own blood. Mykel was alive, thankfully, being restrained by two men in white coats, their faces covered with surgical masks.

She grimaced.

God below, she *hated* the Candle. Not even the Idol gave her the creeps the way the Candle did. And if the orderlies weren't bad enough, the patients were even worse. Standing around the edge of the room, wearing their basic linen pants and long shirts, were the brainless, empty, zombie-like creatures that had once been people.

It was hard to tell if they were living or dead. She suspected it was a mix of both. Their skin was sallow, their lips a grayish purple. Their eyes were cloudy, unfocused, and dim. For all intents and purposes, they would be mistaken for corpses if they weren't standing upright on their own accord.

A dozen or more stood silently around the room. Some

had bloody fingers, likely having killed her people with their bare hands. All on the command of the man who stood in the center of them.

Dr. Thaddeus Kirkbride was an imposing man. Standing well over six feet tall, his height was accentuated by how thin he was. His hair was grayer now than when he had taken over the Asylum so many years ago, and he leaned heavily on a cane. His uniform was like the others, all white, as was the surgical mask that covered his sharp, hawkish features.

"Forgive the intrusion." His voice sounded like a snake moving through grass. Gigi hated it like she hated the rest of him.

"Get out. You have no business here. Are you trying to start a war?" She huffed and waved a hand at Mykel. "This mistreatment—"

"War?" Kirkbride laughed. "I am not here to start a war—I am here to end one."

She bristled at being interrupted. It was her least favorite thing in the world. She tossed her fur stole over her shoulder. "If you think I'll—"

Kirkbride interrupted her a second time. "First, you join forces with the Mirror. That was dangerous enough. But now I hear rumors that you're working with the Bishop! What further proof do I need that you've lost your mind? What further proof do I need that you are in desperate need of treatment?"

Gigi masked her fear behind a look of pure contempt. "The Idol must be stopped. At all costs."

"The first part, yes. I agree with you. But the Idol is easily foiled without such overt, foolish gestures. No, I think you are merely lying to yourself." Thaddeus tilted his head to the side as he watched her. "Your whole life is nothing but lies you tell yourself, isn't it? I can help you accept the truth."

"If you think—"

He snapped his fingers.

Gigi was not a fighter. She had skills. Many skills. But hand-to-hand combat was not on that list. The tiny pistol she pulled from her purse had only just gotten into her hand when it was harshly knocked out of it, sending it skittering to the floor.

"If you dare touch me, you'll—" Hands roughly grasped her, forcing her down to the blood-soaked carpet. "Get off of me, you—" She felt a needle prick the skin of her throat, even as she felt them tear her clothes away to put one of those awful white jackets over her. Her arms were pinned across her now as they yanked the straps of the straitjacket behind her back.

"Don't fight it." Expensive shoes entered her line of sight, even as her head was held down by one of the orderlies. She struggled and kicked as hard as she could, but she felt the thick, viscous liquid push into her through the needle in her throat. "You can't win."

He was right. The warmth was already spreading through her limbs, slowing her down. It felt like she was moving through water, and the harder she pushed, the harder it was to move.

"It will be all right. Your troubles are over. I'll make sure you get the help you need. We can stop your pain."

It was so hard to keep her eyes open. She tried. She tried to keep fighting. She tried to stay awake. But like the cinch of the leather straps now ensuring that she couldn't even move her arms, it was hopeless.

Gigi shut her eyes, and, going limp, she gave up.

EMMA DIDN'T MAKE it far. Not like she expected any less. When the front door was covered by a sea of swarming, wriggling tendrils, she took a left turn into the first-floor study. Maybe she could make it out the back door and into the garden, and—

At least this time, when the shadowy appendage snapped around her ankle, she didn't trip and eat the floor. Instead, she tripped and ate the sofa, grunting as she did.

"I swear," Rafe's voice came from right behind her. He grabbed her by the waist, half throwing, half planting her face-first onto the cushioned surface. "If I didn't know better, I'd say you *like* running away and being caught."

"I need to help Gigi, and—" She gasped as one of those dark, shadowy things wound around her throat. It didn't cinch tight, it didn't stop her breathing—it just stayed there, thick and hot. More of them wrapped around her wrists. They yanked them forward over her head, keeping her from straightening up. Rafe picked her up by her waist again, settling her on her knees, her ass sticking up in the air. "Wait—"

He pushed her dress up around her waist, both his hands now free to roam her body, stroking over the globes of her ass. He grunted, clearly enjoying the view. "What're you going to do? Run head-first into the Asylum, and do what? You'll get captured instantly. If the Candle is working with the Idol, that's it. You're done. And so are the rest of us. No, Emma." He brought a hand down on her ass with a *crack.*

She wailed, trying to squirm away from him. But there was no use.

"We are going to stay right here and wait this all out." He rubbed the offended spot, soothing the stinging skin. "And we're going to have fun while we do it."

"Please, Rafe—" She was cut off as he slapped her ass a second time. She let out a whine, though it ended in a sound that betrayed just how much she was, in truth, enjoying this. *Now's not the time!*

"Remember our rule, pretty girl? You say stop, we stop? You say wait...we keep going." He chuckled. "Well, I'm afraid to say there's only one problem with that rule. One little loophole you might not have caught." He cupped her core, fingers stroking over her, finding out just how very much she was enjoying their game of cat and mouse.

Or monster and victim.

Whatever.

"Which is...which is what?" She bit back a moan.

For a moment, he didn't answer her. He unclipped her garters and pulled her underwear down around her knees. "Simply put." His hand met her now-bare skin a third time.

She opened her mouth to cry out. She didn't get a chance. One of those dark, shadowy things pushed into her mouth, blocking the sound. It was thick and hot, the pointed end of it exploring her, wrapping around her tongue, pressing into every corner as if wanting to touch every part of her.

"You have to be able to speak." Rafe's laugh was one of pure evil. Of pure sin. Of pure *desire.*

When the appendage in her mouth pushed into her throat, she gagged. Rafe's hands were on her ass again, slowly rubbing over her skin. "Don't fight it. Relax. Hold your breath when we go deep and let it happen. We won't hurt you. We won't strangle you. Give up, pretty girl. Give up and let go. We have you."

The tendril pulled out of her throat and let her pull in her breath through her nose. When it drove back in, she did her best to do as Rafe told her. She tried to stay relaxed. It was tapered, and hot, and she could feel the point of it pushing farther as it grew in thickness in her mouth. She could feel it sliding against her tongue. It didn't taste like anything at all.

When it slid back out so she could breathe, she fought the urge to cough.

"You're so perfect, Emma. So wonderfully perfect." He moaned. "I wish you could see yourself right now…"

His fingers found her core again, one of them pushing in deep as he played with her sensitive ball of nerves with his thumb. She moaned as the tendril in her mouth pushed into her throat again.

It shouldn't feel good.

It shouldn't.

But it did.

"There it is…that's it. I can feel you. Give in." Rafe pushed a second finger into her. There were tendrils around her thighs now, squeezing and releasing, writhing higher and higher. She felt more starting to worm their way underneath her dress and undergarments, seeking out her breasts. They were everywhere. Around her ankles, around her waist, around her throat.

What was she supposed to do?

She couldn't fight him. And she couldn't fight how much he made her feel.

And the press of the hot tendril through her mouth and down her throat sparked something vicious and undeniable inside her. Something that demanded *more,* and it demanded it *right now.*

Rafe was right. There wasn't anything she could do to help Gigi. She was completely over her head. The rest of her argument was pushed out of her mind as Rafe redoubled his efforts, his thumb pressing hard to her most sensitive spot, sending flashes of white over her vision as shocks of pleasure rushed over her.

Ecstasy took her, hard and fast, and the tendril in her mouth withdrew enough that she could gasp air into her lungs. When the bliss faded, it left a roaring fire in its wake. He was right. She loved this game. She more than wanted him right now—she needed him.

Monster and all.

She relaxed in his grasp and did as he was urging her to do. She gave up.

"Yes, Emma. *Yes.*" He moaned, plunging three fingers into her to the knuckle. "We can't decide what we want to do first...choices, choices, so many options. Front, back, top, bottom..."

The tendril in her mouth had set a pace, slowly thrusting in and out of her throat and her mouth, sometimes pushing the limit of how long she could hold her breath. She moaned against it, letting her eyes slip shut. It felt so damnably *erotic.* It was hard to deny that it sent waves of pleasure through her each time it pushed deep, its warmth hot and thick against her tongue.

"Well, see, now he's getting jealous! Look at you...you like that, don't you, naughty girl?"

He stood from behind her, and she yelped as the thing in her mouth withdrew all the way, instead using its presence around her throat to straighten her up to her knees. The limbs around her wrists let go of her briefly, and she grabbed at the one around her neck, trying to pull it away "Wait—I—"

"Shush."

She could only frantically grab at the tendril before it shoved itself into her mouth again, taking the opportunity to silence her halfhearted protests.

Rafe sat down in front of her, sitting sideways on the sofa with her between his knees. He had undone his fly and freed himself from his pants. The look on his face was insidious and dark as he leisurely stroked himself with one hand. He let her tug uselessly at the tendril around her neck and inside her throat, as if she could possibly stop it from resuming its tempo.

More of the things took off the rest of her clothes, leaving her in nothing but her stockings. It seemed those could stay.

His eyes were black as the void, and lidded with lust as he stroked his length, watching her. "So beautiful...so perfect."

Muffled, she let out a *mmfhn!* as the tendrils pulled her forward, doubling her over. She hit her elbows on either side of his waist, her face perfectly lined up with...well, yeah. They'd warned her Rafe was getting jealous.

"He's wanted to shut you up like this since the day he met you. Do you know that? Oh, he wanted to bend you over his desk in the middle of that lecture hall and fuck your ever-loving brains out." He chuckled darkly. "Metaphorically, of course."

He tangled his hand into her hair. The tendril left her mouth with a pop. "You insuff—" Her insult was cut off as he pushed himself—at least a different part of himself, she supposed—into her mouth, silencing her yet again.

Their moans twisted together as he leaned his head back, thrusting his hips up into her mouth. "Emma, yes...please, Emma...be good for me, please?"

The request came as a surprise. She supposed she did have a choice. She could bite down. She could scream and cry and make him stop.

But she wanted to do none of those things.

She shut her eyes and relaxed in his grip once more.

Perfect. Ours. Yes! Yes, forever. Ours, forever!

Rafe couldn't tear his eyes away from the delicious sight in front of him. In front of *them*. He was in more control than he let on. Or that he wanted to admit to Emma. It was true, what they had said. He had wanted to shut her up with his cock between her lips since he set eyes on her.

And now, there she was. Although not perhaps entirely how he would have predicted.

He urged her head lower, and she obeyed. He pressed his hips up into her and gave her some time to acclimate herself. He was thicker than the appendage he had prepared her with. But he knew how to inspire her.

The tendrils were all around her, writhing and squeezing, twisting and exploring. Toying with her breasts, playing with her nipples—tugging on them painfully enough that she would twitch and whimper.

Last time, he had barely stretched her with their presence. He hadn't wanted to frighten her. Last time had purely been about dipping her toes in the water. This time, however, she was ready for more.

He waited until he pushed himself into her throat, snarling in pleasure as her tight, volcanic body clenched down on him, before he allowed one of the tendrils to do the same to her core. It slid inside, the taper quickly growing thicker as it squirmed into her willing flesh.

She pulled her head back, breaking free of him, wailing as a second, and then a third, and then a fourth quickly joined the first as they drove into her body. "Oh—oh, God—"

"Not here. Just us. Although…we're close enough, wouldn't you say?" He ran a finger along her lower lip, loving the sight of her, eyes shut, gasping for air, brow pinched in overwhelming sensation.

Normal mortal sex was so boring, wasn't it? In, out, in, out, in, out. They imagined it must get terribly repetitive. They could do both at the same time, they could coil together, they could explore her. Touch the parts that felt the best. Torment her. Stretch her to just the right point. They could *fill* her.

She was shaking, her body slowly coating itself in a thin sheen of sweat. "Rafe, I—ah! Please, wait, I—"

"Nope. You know the rules. Back to work, pretty girl." He laughed as he pushed her head down onto him. He loved the feeling of forcing his way inside. Of feeling her brief struggle and sweet surrender as she quickly gave in. He set a good tempo, thrusting deep into her throat every few strokes, going just a little deeper than before, wanting to see if she could take him all. He was betting she could. He was betting he was going to find out.

Now and then, he stopped to let her breathe as the pleasure became too much for her and she was overcome. "Breathe deep, pretty girl." He pressed himself deep into her mouth again and urged her to go farther, farther, just a little farther…

Her nose touched his body, and he couldn't help it. He thrusted his hips up to meet her, holding her head there with both his hands. He roared. The weak mortal body couldn't take it. He exploded in her throat, wave after wave of something unlike anything they had ever felt crashing over them.

Oh. Now we get it. This wasn't boring.

She slapped his thigh, bringing him back to reality. Pulling himself out of her body, he shuddered and twitched in the aftermath. She was panting, her chest heaving, her head resting against his abdomen.

She seemed at her wits' end, having been brought to climax several times already. He watched her, wanting to bring her to one more peak. It didn't take long, and he drank in the sight of her as another wave of pleasure sent her crashing over the cliffs.

When she descended, he stilled, pulling the tendrils from her, using only a few to carefully pull her up his body to lie against his chest. He held her close, wrapping his arms around her, kissing her forehead.

"Hate you," she murmured into his shirt.

"You don't mean that." He smiled. "I suppose I should be the one to make breakfast now, hm?"

She groaned.

He laughed.

This wasn't boring at all.

"Soon, we'll be together forever, Emma. Doesn't that sound divine? You will become us, and we will never be apart." He shut his eyes, smiling peacefully.

We think we're in love. How novel.

EMMA TOOK A SHOWER, lost deep in thought, as "Rafe" cooked breakfast. Maybe the line between the professor and Them was only blurry because she wanted it to be. Maybe it was gone the moment she had shot him. Maybe she had only quickened the inevitable.

She knew she couldn't save Gigi. At least, not on her own. Maybe the Bishop would help her. Or she could track down Yuriel again. He seemed like a noble whatever-the-fuck. But she did know one thing.

She had no interest in becoming like Rafe. She had no interest in becoming part of Them. Staring at herself in the mirror after dressing, she noticed the slight bruise forming on the edge of her throat by her collarbone.

It had felt incredible. The things They could do to her were unnatural but astonishing. She wanted Them, just as badly as she wanted Rafe. She brushed her fingers along the slowly darkening yellow spot. It wasn't a bad mark, and she'd had far worse in her day. And it'd been worth it.

But was the rest of it worth it? She cared about Rafe. The more she thought about it, the more obvious it was becoming that she more than cared about him. She loved him. And if she wasn't mistaken…she was starting to fall in love with Them, too. *They're the same thing, now, after all.*

But They ate people. And it was only a matter of time

before They ate her. They were just willing to wait longer for her than the rest.

I don't know if there's an afterlife. I don't know if there's really a Benevolent God waiting for me. Or if I'll ever see Elliot or Momma again. But she did know one thing. She didn't want to be another voice in the legion that was the writhing void.

She knew what she had to do.

Even if she hated it.

If she couldn't run? Well…

Then she only had one other option.

CHAPTER TWENTY-TWO

Patrick paced his office, back and forth, back and forth, back and forth. Everything felt wrong. Everything felt *terrible*. He knew he shouldn't spare a thought over Gigi's fate. She was a cultist. She was a criminal. She stood for everything he stood against.

And it was only a matter of time before she ascended in power and had to be…dealt with. The idea of having to remove her from the board made his stomach churn.

Sinking down into the chair at his desk, he put his hand over his eyes. What could he do? He couldn't storm the Asylum.

Well, all right, he *could*.

But Kirkbride was heavily connected. It'd cause a chain reaction and likely create a power vacuum in the man's absence. Sometimes, killing one monster only allowed a bigger, more dangerous one to take its place.

Perhaps he could be reasoned with. Perhaps he could negotiate for Gigi's release. *No. That's suicide. Revealing any kind of connection between us could put us both at risk.* If his Church learned that he had any sort of relations with a cultist, he'd be put on trial or immediately hanged for his crime.

Leaning back in the chair, he heard the familiar creak of the wood. There was nothing he could do to save Gigi. Nothing at all.

Maybe it was for the best.

Maybe this solved his problem. *Don't get sentimental, priest.* It was very good advice. Advice that he, like a fool, was slowly realizing he had no way of following.

It was too late.

GIGI KEPT her head held high as they tightened the leather restraints that kept her strapped to the thin, white chair. She couldn't move her arms or legs. And another strap around her chest kept her from moving more than an inch in any direction.

She didn't care. That was the easiest way to win—not caring.

She didn't care about the buzz of the electric razor as they sheared her head like she was nothing but livestock. She didn't even flinch as the prongs caught her scalp and cut her. It was meant to demoralize her, she knew. Their excuse about *lice* was nonsense.

Her body meant nothing. It was mutable. Once she was free, and once Kirkbride paid for this indignity, everything could be mended.

She smiled and kept her head held high. And reminded herself that soon all the orderlies and nurses in this forsaken place would be dead. That she would carry the gasoline and light the match herself that burned the damnable asylum to the ground. She hadn't lied when she had told Patrick that she had never once murdered anyone.

As a point of fact, she found it a very crude and childish way to solve problems. There was always a better way around issues than brute force.

But for Kirkbride, she was going to make an exception.

Just as soon as she had the chance.

The room she was in was painted a hideous shade of yellowish green. She was sure it was meant to be calming, but it reminded her too much of vomit for it to do anything of the sort. The floor was tile that had once been white, but now revealed that white floors were always a terrible idea. All the grit and grime—and blood—had gathered in the grout, turning it various shades of brown and black.

The door in front of her clicked open. It was a heavy metal thing, clearly designed to withstand all attempts at escape. The small, circular window in the middle was covered with glass that had been molded with a wire mesh, making it feel even more prison-like, not that it much needed the help.

The man who stepped inside earned a sneer from her as he entered.

Kirkbride.

He was still wearing his surgical mask. It made him look even more freakish. His long coat was immaculate and pristine, the shade the floor tiles had probably been the day they were placed.

"How are you feeling today?" Kirkbride asked as he eyed her narrowly.

"You have no power to keep me here. Let me go, Thaddeus, and I'll do what I can to forgive your little indiscretion." She smiled. She didn't bother to pull at the leather restraints. What would be the point?

"I have every right." He leaned on the cane at his side. From what Gigi knew of him, he had been in a train accident at some point in his life and was slightly lame in one leg. The cane helped him move, but she also suspected he enjoyed the drama of it all. "You are clinically unwell. And I am charged, by the grace of the mayor of this city, to help those who cannot help themselves."

Laughing, she shook her head. "And how, precisely, am I 'clinically unwell' in any way that you don't share with me, Thaddeus?" She was certain the orderly who was sweeping up her blonde locks from the floor was fully aware of Kirkbride's darker pursuits.

Some organizations could operate in full daylight, as long as they only hurt those who couldn't complain or fight back. The poor, the destitute, the ill—no one cared about what happened to them. They weren't really human, after all.

Kirkbride *tsk*ed before letting out a disappointed sigh. "You are in such deep denial that you truly don't see it, do you? That's all right. We'll work on that. Don't worry, we'll help you come to terms with your illness. Soon, you won't even have to lie to yourself."

"Lie to myself about *what*, precisely?" She laughed. "I'm not the one in denial, 'doctor.' Tell me something—are the rumors true? Do you spend your nights here diddling your patients?" She sneered up at him. "You like the ones who can't fight back, eh? Get them all nice and drugged up, all nice and docile…"

"Sling your insults and insinuations all you like. It matters not to me." He walked over to a table by the wall. On it were several metal trays. Lifting a syringe from one, he reached into his coat pocket to pull out a vial of liquid. The contents were dark and muddy looking. It was completely opaque, the substance moving slowly as he flipped it upside down and inserted the end of the syringe through the cap.

She frowned. "What is that?"

"Nothing to be concerned about."

"No. You are going to tell me what that is. You're going to

tell me what you're going to do to me!" She yanked on the restraints for the first time. It was as pointless as she figured it was going to be.

"Very well. I suppose as a fellow…*high-climbing* individual, who understands the true workings of the world, I will tell you." He turned to face her now that the syringe was filled with the thick, sludge-like substance. "This drug is how we treat all my…deeply ill patients here at Arnsmouth Asylum."

No. No, no, no! She thrashed. She would not become one of those things, one of those lifeless, soulless carcasses that wandered his halls and answered his bidding. "Don't you *dare* put that shit in me, you—"

He gestured to the orderly, who quickly went to work. Snatching her face painfully, he forced her mouth open. She screamed as the man crammed a wooden dowel into her mouth, wrapped in a scrap of leather, and secured it around her shaved head with a tie.

Muffled, all she could do was scream, and scream, and scream. She kicked and thrashed. But it was of no use. She was trapped.

Trapped and alone.

And now she was afraid.

"Shush." Kirkbride didn't hesitate as he cleaned a spot on her arm with a wipe covered in alcohol, the scent stinging her nose. It only deepened her growing sense of panic. "This is only your first dose. Hopefully, you won't need many more."

She could only watch, helpless, as Kirkbride shoved the needle in her arm. It stung, and she snarled loudly in rage as he depressed the plunger. She expected it to burn. She expected to feel something rip through her like lightning.

Instead, she felt…warm.

Shaking her head, she tried to fight it. Tried to stop the cloud that was settling over her. Tried to resist how…good it made her feel. Everything tingled. The world felt softer. The pain from the restraints vanished. The uncomfortable little chair could have been made of a cloud.

She felt the tension in her limbs begin to loosen.

Her panic was gone. Her fear was gone.

And with it went all of her worries. The walls were such a wonderful color. They reminded her of spring grass. Of freedom.

She was free.

"There we go." He rubbed her forearm, soothing the spot, working the thick sludge into her veins. "You're in good hands, Gregory. Soon, you'll be walking out of here, cured of your disease and a better man than you were before."

The use of her old name jarred her out of her daze. Sleepily, unable to really hold on to the world around her, she looked up at Kirkbride. How did the doctor know? Nobody knew...nobody had called her that name in twenty years.

Gregory was buried and gone.

She'd murdered him. He was dust.

But that was the power of the Candle, wasn't it? The power over life and death. The power to raise corpses and set them out into the world with a new purpose—*Kirkbride's* purpose.

And he wanted to bring Gregory back from the dead.

She should be terrified.

Absolutely *terrified*.

But all she could think to herself was how very sleepy she was.

"You're safe, Mr. Gage." Kirkbride placed a hand on her shoulder. "Get some rest. When you wake up, we will begin your treatment."

Someone...help me.

Rafe stood beside the stove, staring down at the skillet. He was making grilled cheese. He wasn't sure what else to make with the limited supplies he had. He wasn't used to having company, let alone being expected to cook for said company.

And the voices in his head would not *shut up* about it.

We really should learn to go grocery shopping. How is it that we're a grown man and don't know how to properly grocery shop?

I can grocery shop just fine.

Your pantry begs otherwise.

I don't need your advice, thank you very much.

We think you do. We should learn to properly feed ourselves. And now we should learn to cook for her, too.

Why?

You know why.

I really don't.

Because we love her. And it's a nice gesture.

Shutting his eyes, he whacked his forehead on the cupboard.

"That doesn't help, y'know." Emma chuckled sadly as she walked into the room. "Trust me. I'm speaking from experience."

"I dislike how incessant they are." He flipped the grilled cheese over. It was only slightly overcooked. He kept his back to her, not daring to take his eyes off the food. It took his full attention to cook the sandwiches. *Fine, yes, I could improve my cooking skills.*

Told you.

He winced.

"I don't blame you." She paused. "At least the voices in my head aren't real. They're just my faulty 'wiring.' I don't have… unknowable terrors living inside my mind."

"Honestly, I would prefer it if they were simply a delusion. It would make the consequences far less threatening." He frowned. He had heard every word he had said to her as they had made love. And he knew the Things inside him wouldn't stop until they had made good on their threat to consume her.

It's a promise. And why wouldn't she want to join us? We will be together forever. One second, he was terrified at the notion, and in the next, it calmed him. The man he had once been was horrified at the idea that they were both doomed to become part of the writhing, fathomless darkness. But the man he now was, tangled up in it already, wanted to hold her close and ensure they were never parted.

It all made him want to get very deeply drunk.

"I want to go save Gigi. I want to get her out of the asylum. They're going to torture her there, or worse. She's been a friend to me—to *us*—and we should help her."

"No." He sighed. "I'm sorry. Her fate is her own. We should never have involved ourselves with her. And going to the asylum is suicide. Kirkbride is exceedingly dangerous, and if he's working with the Idol, we can't risk it."

Emma went silent as she thought it over. "What about the Bishop? He could help."

"He won't. Nor should we be involved with *him,* either. The instructions were to lay low, and that's what we need to do."

"I need to find someone who will help her. I'll go get Mykel. She has to have other allies."

"You are *not* leaving my home. Not under any circumstances." He regretted how cold he sounded. Shoulders slumping, he tried again. "I'm sorry, Emma. I'm sorry for what will become of Gigi. I'm sorry about all of this. About what I've become, about…them." He shook his head. "I can't stop them. I *am* them now, and I…"

"It's all right. It isn't your fault."

"I may not be fully to blame, but I am entirely responsible." He felt the muscle in his jaw twitch as he scraped the sandwiches out of the pan and put them on plates before flipping off the gas. "I chased knowledge that I knew was forbidden. I chased power, and when it was just my own life and soul at risk, it didn't matter to me. But now that you're mixed up in all this, I can't stand the idea of…" He shut his eyes. "Emma, I…"

Tell her, you moron.

He couldn't tell which part of him that had come from. It didn't matter. Grimacing, he gave up hiding the truth that so many others had already seen. "I love you, Emma."

She was silent for a long moment. With each tick of the clock, he felt a noose tighten around his heart.

"I love you, too, Rafe."

He hadn't realized he had been holding his breath. Letting out a rush of air, he turned to her and smiled, and—

She swung something at his head.

The world went dark.

CHAPTER TWENTY-THREE

Emma stood there, staring down at Rafe. Her grasp on the fire poker had her knuckles turning white. Rafe wasn't moving. His eyes were open, glassy, and unseeing. And there was a pool of blood forming around him like a sick halo.

The blood was *black*.

A reminder of what he really was.

Choking out a sob, she felt like she was going to retch. Taking a step back, she leaned against the doorjamb.

Rafe was a monster. A monster that wanted to *eat her whole*. One that would murder Yuriel to keep her safe. One that would devour the whole world and then her soul.

One that she loved.

"I'd feel worse, y'know, if I didn't feel fully confident that you're going to get back up," she murmured to his corpse. She wiped a hand over her eyes. "You're going to be mad. I'm sorry." Sniffling, she committed herself to what she had to do.

No, she wasn't going to go to the asylum by herself. She

knew he was right. Once she stepped in there, she'd never come back out. But someone had to help Gigi.

Walking outside, she turned and locked the door behind her. She'd stolen Rafe's house keys a long while ago. Turning, she yelped as she walked straight into someone. They grabbed her shoulders to keep them both from toppling over.

He laughed. "Hey, there, little girl. Just the one I was coming to see."

She blinked and then furrowed her brow. It took her a second to recognize him. The street urchin who had found her in the tunnels under the city. "Robert? What're you—"

"I'm going to go out on a limb and say you want to help Gigi." He glanced down at her hand. "And you plan on rescuing her with a fire poker?"

"I—uh—" Honestly, she hadn't realized she was still holding it. "Not really. I don't actually have a plan."

"Perfect." He half-hopped down the stairs to the sidewalk. "Because I do! C'mon, kid. Let's go rescue the jazz singer."

She knew she shouldn't trust Robert. She knew he was playing every possible angle to get ahead. She knew his type and knew he was probably four steps ahead and had already sold her out to the highest bidder. She stood there, glaring at him.

With a sigh, he shrugged. "Fine. No harm in telling you. Kirkbride wants to talk to you. That's all. Just talk."

"Bullshit."

"I'm not kidding!" He folded his arms over his thin chest. He was a skinny thing. "He wants to meet you. Just that. To talk about your situation, and how we can all get past this *Mather* problem together." He jerked his head toward the door. "Something tells me you and the professor just broke up."

"That's one way to put it."

Robert snickered. "I like you. I really do. And I'm not just saying that. Can you trust me? No. Can you trust Kirkbride? No. But you also don't have any other choices."

"I'm going to go talk to the Bishop. He's reasonable. He'll help me." She started walking in the other direction, heading toward the Church of the Benevolent God. She didn't know if Patrick Caner was there, but she would wait for him.

"Is he?" Robert chuckled as he jogged to catch up with her, falling in step beside her. "He's not what he seems, kid. He's got just as many secrets as the rest of us, if not more. Besides, he can't help Gigi."

"First of all, you don't know that. And second, he can't, or won't?" She hated everything about everything right now, and Robert pestering her really wasn't helping.

"Hm. Fair. He won't. You really think he wants to let the world know that he and Gigi were, as rumor has it..." He created an O with his pointer finger and thumb on one hand and shoved the pointer finger of his other hand into it. He grinned.

She rolled her eyes. Men. "And?"

"If word gets out that he's having relations with one of his enemies...you really think the rest of his Church will take kindly to that? He's just a Bishop. They'll hang him in the public square to set an example." Robert grimaced. "He—" He shut up as they passed an Investigator that was standing at the corner, their masked face turning to follow them as they went by.

The Investigators still gave her the creeps.

"Fuckin' cult," Robert muttered after they were out of earshot.

For some reason, it made her laugh. When he smiled at her, she realized that was entirely the point. She shook her head. "I'll go see Mykel, then. He'll help get Gigi out, and he'll know who else is willing to get involved. Do you know where he is?"

"Probably at the Flesh & Bone, I imagine." Robert shrugged. "Last I knew."

"Then, fine. That's where I'm going." She changed directions abruptly, leaving Robert to stagger and jog after her again. "Alone."

"No, I'm coming." Robert shrugged, shoving his hands into his tattered coat pockets. "You're where all the action is, and I'm going to follow the action."

"Why?" She arched an eyebrow at him.

"One, I'm getting paid to."

She groaned.

"Two." He grinned. "I think this is going to be fun."

"I deeply dislike you, Robert." She glared at him, knowing it was useless. He was going to follow her, and she couldn't do anything to stop him.

That only made him laugh. "Join the club, kid. Join the club."

I'm not sure how any of this can get any worse, but I get the feeling I'm going to find out.

EMMA DIDN'T SAY a word the entire walk to the club. That didn't mean they were walking in silence, however. Robert never seemed to shut up—and coming from her, that was a trick. He filled every scrap of available silence with some random story or tale about "that time the ship came in with plague rats" or when he "found himself on the wrong end of a bad deal."

He omitted all the names from his stories, instead substituting them with things like "we'll call him Harry" or "let's say her name was Amanda."

Whatever.

She just wanted him to shut up.

When they reached the club, she instantly knew something had gone very, very wrong inside. The front door was off its hinges, stuck wide open. She froze. She knew Gigi was gone, but…seeing the aftermath was something else entirely.

"I'll stay here. You can poke around to your heart's content." He snickered. Leaning up against the brick wall beside the entrance, he pulled out a cigarette and shoved it between his lips.

That was probably for the best. Carefully, her hand on her gun in her purse, she stepped inside the club. Everything was *wrecked.* Tables and chairs were flipped. Curtains were torn off the walls. Lights were shattered, and bits of broken glass lay scattered about on the ground amidst dark stains. Some might be from spilled drinks.

Some were definitely from blood.

"Mykel?" Silence. "Anybody?"

Damn. Damn, damn, damn.

There was no one there. Deflated, she went to leave and pulled up her steps as something on the wall caught her eye.

It was a symbol, drawn on the wall in blood with the swipe of a few fingers. The symbol of the Great Beast. And there, taped to the wall beside it, was a letter, folded in thirds.

She knew it was addressed to her even before she saw her name written neatly on it. Pulling it from the wall, she flipped it open and read the tidy script she now recognized as belonging to Dr. Kirkbride.

"Dear Emma,

In case my previous letter did not reach you, as I am sure Professor Saltonstall saw fit to intercept it, allow me to plead my case once more. I am not your enemy. Your brother is salvageable—

the Idol's fanaticism is medical, not mystical. He is merely in a trance. I can cure him.

And if you are concerned for your 'friend' Gage, you do not know who it is you are truly worried over.

I have no intention of surrendering you to the Idol. I have no taste for their zealous desire for destruction. I also have no intention of imprisoning you. Your illness is benign to you and is therefore of no interest to my work. I implore you—come speak to me. Upon my word, I promise you will be free to leave the asylum once you enter.

Your friend,
    Dr. Thaddeus Kirkbride"

She knew it was bullshit. She knew it was a crock of lies. What was she going to do, take on a cult with a pistol and a fire poker?

Shutting her eyes, she wanted to give up. Wanted to just curl up in a corner and cry. She knew in her heart that Kirkbride was wrong about Yuriel. Her brother was dead and gone. She had seen it in the man's eyes.

Maybe it's better if I'm dead. Maybe it's better if I just give up and jump off a bridge. It seems I cause more trouble than good no matter where I go. Rafe is a monster because of me. Gigi is being tortured because of me. Who knows what other mayhem and pain I'll cause, the longer I'm alive?

It was all hopeless. If she hid with Rafe, he'd consume her. He'd turn her into a thing like him. If she ran away, she knew the city would just find a way to pull her back. And if she went to see Kirkbride…at least she might stand a chance of helping Gigi.

Even if it was clearly a trap.

Emma was still wiping at her tears as she walked back out of the club, the doctor's letter shoved in her pocket.

"Well?" Robert stomped out what remained of his cigarette beneath his shoe. "Find anybody?"

"No."

"Could've warned you."

Heading off down the street, she tried not to grimace as Robert fell in step beside her. She tried and failed. "Go away, Robert."

"Nah. Said why. Besides, I know where you're going now." He smiled, a sickly-sweet thing that made her skin crawl. "You're going to see Kirkbride. Because you finally understand you're out of options. Anyway, so, the story we left off with, I was—"

"Robert, if you don't shut up, I'm going to shove this fire poker up your ass." She shook it at him.

He cackled. "Threaten me with a good time!" Letting out a thoughtful hum, he scratched his chin. "You know someone got assassinated that way once. A King, too. So, as the story goes, I think—"

Emma groaned.

Now she really *was* praying for death.

RAFE PUSHED himself up onto his hands and knees, groaning at the pain that was splitting his skull open.

Well, that's accurate. It was.

Everything in his body ached. But his head felt oddly clear, even through the pain. It was like his view had… zoomed out. It was hard to describe. He could simply see the bigger picture now, and it made him smile.

There was a song playing through his head, played to the tick of a metronome. Or perhaps it was a clock. He loved the feel of it, melancholy as it was, and couldn't help but hum along. He knew the song might never leave his head now. But that was all right. He enjoyed it and somehow knew it would never get irritating.

Kneeling, he ran a hand through his hair, wincing as it came back covered in thick blood the color of pitch. It should have alarmed him, watching his humanity slip away bit by bit, blow by blow. *Bullet by bullet and wound by wound.*

Emma.

He laughed. He laughed hard. Finally getting to his feet, he staggered and hit the counter. It took him a few seconds to get his legs under him. Walking away, he leaned on the walls, leaving smears of that black ichor behind. He didn't care.

"That girl really needs to stop murdering us." He chuckled again.

She'll march right into that asylum and get herself into deep trouble. So, you know what we have to do, right?

Kill them all.

Kill every last single person in this damned city if we have to. Eat them all, send them to the void, and reign supreme. Rise to Sainthood and ensure that nobody will ever lay a hand on her again.

Nobody but us.

It sounded like a fantastic plan. He'd go after Emma and save her, and in doing so, start with murdering Kirkbride. Then Gigi. Then Yuriel. Then Tudor Gardner and the whole of the Idol. Then the Bishop. He would rid the city of all the other Dark Societies.

One, by one, by one, he'd consume them all.

The knock on the door was loud enough that he swore under his breath. All right, it probably wasn't *that* loud, but he had a splitting headache. When the knock came again, harder and angrier than before, he stormed up to the front door and threw it open. *"What?"*

The man on the other side glowered at him, unfazed by his shouted and rude greeting. "Professor Saltonstall."

It was Dean James Toppan.

Rafe stifled a laugh and settled for a grin that was likely a bit wolfish. He didn't care. He felt rather wolfish. He also felt rather starving.

"You have missed a solid week of classes. You haven't called, haven't answered your phone, and all attempts to reach you other than showing up to your damn door have failed." The Dean smirked, clearly very proud of himself. "This gives me every excuse to fire you. I should have done it long ago, with all the rumors circulating about your...*involvements* with blasphemous—" He paused. "What is that on your face? Ink? Are you bleeding? What's happened to you, man?"

"Hm?" Rafe touched his temple. Oh, he was still bleeding. Charming. "You've always been so clever, Dean, finding me out where no one else was smart or brave enough." He sighed mournfully. "Come in, sit down. Let me explain everything." Rafe stepped aside, gesturing for him to enter.

Triumphant, the fool stomped past him inside his home. "I have a gun, by the way. I have no problem shooting you if you try any funny business, Saltonstall." Toppan glanced at every object he passed, as if Rafe was stupid enough to keep any of his valuable artifacts out in the open.

"I promise you I won't try anything *funny*." Rafe shut the door and locked it. Grinning, he walked back toward the Dean. "I don't think you'll find this funny at all."

He let his darkness uncoil. He let the hunger loose.

The Dean might not find it amusing. But Rafe found it *hysterical.*

Step One, save the idiot girl who won't stop murdering us.

Step Two...kill everyone else.
This is going to be fun.
Toppan screamed.
Rafe laughed.
A great deal of fun, indeed.

TO BE CONTINUED IN BOOK THREE OF

TENEBRIS: AN OCCULT ROMANCE

"Of Grave & Glory"

ABOUT THE AUTHOR

Kat has always been a storyteller.

With ten years in script-writing for performances on both the stage and for tourism, she has always been writing in one form or another. When she isn't penning down fiction, she works as Creative Director for a company that designs and builds large-scale interactive adventure games. There, she is the lead concept designer, handling everything from game and set design, to audio and lighting, to illustration and script writing.

Also on her list of skills are artistic direction, scenic painting and props, special effects, and electronics. A graduate of Boston University with a BFA in Theatre Design, she has a passion for unique, creative, and unconventional experiences.

Printed in Great Britain
by Amazon